By Genni Bee

Author's Note

Hey readers,

You're about to read one of my steamy novellas, complete with very mature situations, curse words, some mild stalking danger and more than a few uses of the word cock.

If you are here for the spice and an almost-instalove romance…this is the right book for you.

All the best,
Genni Bee

Chapter 1

Asher

There were exactly fifty-six tiny navy diamonds stitched on Stephen Salman's dove gray tie. They each winked at me, drawing my attention as I stood silently across the room from the corporate executive. I shook my head a fraction of an inch, but it might as well have been a full body shake for all that Stephen's wide, fear-filled gaze flew to me for the hundredth time that day.

I sighed, settling into my heels once more and giving the overanxious gray-haired man a small nod.

He was fine. After all, the only danger we were currently in was being bored to death by this international financier who had been droning on for over an hour.

Something about mergers and big-dollar jobs. I didn't register most of it. In my line of work, I only needed to know what was most important: how to keep my client breathing. At least that's what my brother and father had always preached when we had founded AXE Securities. I'd only been in college when I'd been drafted in for my first case, escorting a high-ranking military official around Chicago.

From the first moment that man placed his trust in my hands, I'd been sold. This was what I was meant to be, what I was meant to do. Since then I'd built myself around that principal. I was born to protect people, and I was damned good at it. I wasn't the only one, either. My brothers were just as devoted, but as our company grew, my brothers were forced from the field to the desk life.

I made sure that my stance on that same fate befalling me was very clear. No fucking way.

I was a field guy. I always would be. And since my older brothers were more than happy to hold the fort from a paperwork standpoint, we were all able to enjoy the work. Even as success came down on us like an avalanche.

But that was years ago now. At this point we were a well-oiled machine, employing a wide variety of bodyguards who would fit the upscale needs of our clientele. And while Dad was partially retired, Emerson thrived at the helm, and I had stayed on the job where I belonged.

My older brother, the middle of our trio, had just been lured back to AXE with the promise of a "normal" schedule in deference to his fiancée's growing baby bump. I was happy for both Emerson and Xavier, but I wasn't ready. Not yet. Hell, maybe not ever.

Still, they persisted. Emerson had an office all set up for me. He wanted me to be head of operations or something and had his email set up to email me an automated job offer every three months. The man took persistence to a whole new level. I still wasn't sure how to explain to him that this was where I belonged. This was where I was the best asset to the company.

"And who are you supposed to be?" The high-pitched voice drew my attention from where I had been scanning the narrow hallway outside of the office.

I lazily looked back to the financier who had turned in his chair to pin me with an assessing look. Mr. Salman shifted behind his desk; his pale skin turned ruddy.

"This is my bodyguard, Asher Brooks."

The financier wrinkled his nose at me, making him look even more like a rodent of some kind. I mentally calculated how easily it would be to chuck him out of the office.

Too easy.

"I can't believe you went through with it. I thought he was just an exotic administrative assistant or something."

I grunted, spreading my feet wide and secretly relishing the way that the financier flinched away from my move. He could talk a big game, but I ate little men like him for breakfast.

"My wife, she seems quite intent on putting me in danger throughout our divorcee proceedings. Mr. Brooks is the best in the company, and he's going to be with me until the papers are signed."

"Or she succeeds," the other man mumbled unhappily.

"Tread carefully, as I'm trained to seek out and resolve any threats." I turned my head slightly, a slow smile curling my lips. "That includes you, sir."

The man sputtered, staring between Mr. Salman and me. "I'm clearly no danger to him."

"Good." I paused to stare over at Mr. Salman. "Glad that we have that confirmed, then."

The meeting concluded shortly after that, and it stroked my ego like none other that both men gave me a wide berth as they walked out into the hallway. I fell into step behind them, my gaze keen on Mr. Salman's back as we made our way through the building and out to the waiting SUV. Somewhere on the first floor, we lost our financier friend, which only made my job more enjoyable.

Mr. Salman wasn't so bad, if you took away the fact that his wife was trying to off him. I suspected that he'd cheated and gotten in over his head with a mistress, but that was just because of my many years of experience in the industry. Emerson never included the reason for the security need unless it had direct ramifications for my work.

I preferred not to know if they had done something wrong. That way I could continue to believe that I was morally sound, when in reality I doubted it every day.

I was good at my job.

That's all I needed to be.

I dropped Mr. Salman off at his house. My colleague Joey Meyer would take the night shift. Now I could go home to my beautiful, oversized apartment, soak up the silence in my leather recliner, and play video games until my eyes bled.

Because Asher Brooks did what he wanted.

**

Lillian

I clutched Tiffany's hand closer, feeling the slick sweat as it bloomed between our hands. It was different, no longer that sweet bout of nerves that sometimes struck my dearest friend and me before we took the stage for performances. This was darker, more severe, and set my heart to racing.

"Do you think he's gone?" Her voice was breathless, and she clutched her flute case close to her chest as we pressed against the exit to the parking garage.

I shook my head, unsure. When I'd made Tiffany promise to let me walk her to her car, I had no idea that it had meant this. Her stalker had always kept his distance, seemingly preferring to send her elaborate love letters and recordings of her practicing her music. But tonight, when we'd opened the parking garage door, still riding the high from our evening performance, we'd seen her car, the bright-blue four-door sedan spray painted with heavy black letters.

"Whore," Tiffany read, her voice thick with fear.

I yanked my phone out, immediately dialed 9-1-1 with shaking fingers, and handed the phone to Tiffany.

"Tell them where we are." I swallowed hard, willing the moisture back to my throat. It was nearly painful to speak. "I'll go look around the side. If he's there, then we'll know."

Tiffany stared at me, bug-eyed. I snorted, realizing how stupid of an idea that probably was. But she followed my directions, pressing the ringing phone to her ear and then reeling off the address of the conservatory parking garage a moment later. I wished with my entire soul that I'd been able to do that, but I'd only been in town a few weeks and had no idea what the address was.

I barely knew north from west most days. Which was embarrassing enough, considering I was almost twenty-three, but in this situation, it was the actual worst.

I toed out of my heels, my feet exposed and naked against the cool concrete. I ducked low, my petite figure doing me a favor as I slowly approached the vandalized sedan.

Behind me, Tiffany had stopped speaking. Hopefully that meant that the police were on their way, because there was no way that I was the best person for this job.

I was a performer, a flute player by profession. I played Mozart and worshipped Lizzo. I did not chase vandals or stalkers, or at least I hadn't before this moment. And I was already regretting it. Deeply.

"Hello," I said softly. I was almost close enough that I'd be able to peek around the side of the car and see if the person remained there. Close enough I could taste the relief at having completed this insane task.

Just as my eyes were able to see around the edge of the car, I saw a tall, darkly dressed man lurch to his feet. My stomach fell straight through my body, and fear turned my mouth sour. I was face-to-face with the man—no, the creature—who had been haunting Tiffany for months. Against all odds and improbability, he had stayed after his "artwork" had been completed.

Stayed and seen me.

My mouth dropped open wide, and for a long, frozen moment, we stared at each other. Then my adrenaline spiked in my throat, and I turned to run, my toes burning against the harsh concrete.

"Run, Tiffany! Get help!" I screamed, my voice echoing off the walls of the garage as my feet scrambled to get away. I was closer to the other exit now, so I turned my entire attention to getting there and getting there as quickly as my legs could carry me.

I was fit. I was young. I would make it. I chanted this in my head over and over again as I tore across the yellow-painted spaces.

The terrifying reality of the footsteps pounding behind me only egged me on, knowing that not only had I seen him, but he was pursuing me. White-hot fear lanced through my mind. He was so much larger than me. And I knew what he had written in those letters. Who knows what he could be capable of doing if he caught me.

Ahead of me, the enclosed stairway's exit door loomed large and gray.

Almost there, I promised myself, lying. *Please, someone, help,* I mentally screamed as my toes tore and legs ached from my racing steps.

When I was only forty or so feet away from my goal, the door opened wide and the entire doorframe was suddenly filled with another man, suited in black and white and pressing a cell phone to his ear.

Behind him, a well-dressed, slender gray-haired man followed like a shadow. Guests from our performance tonight, they had to be. If I could just get to them, they would help me. They would have to. Hope swirled in the muscles in my legs, and I pushed harder.

"Help," I tried to yell, but my empty lungs only whimpered out part of the word. Clenching my fists, I demanded my body keep going, and as the dark-suited man noticed me, he shoved the older man to the ground behind him and spread his legs wide in front of him. I realized that he was my only option, my only answer.

A few feet from the suited man, who I could now see had slightly shaggy black hair and wide dark eyes, I dared to look behind me.

I didn't see my pursuer anymore, but that didn't stop the fear from riding me ever harder. Unwilling to change my stride, I waited until I was only a few feet from my savior

8

before I launched myself into the air, a desperate plea for help still on my lips.

Incredibly hard arms snapped closed around me, and before I had a moment to wrap myself farther around him, I was towed back into the stairway. I glanced down, noting that my mystery savior had also grabbed the collar of the older man and dragged us both against the wall, behind the door we'd come through.

"I-I—" I tried to speak, but instead, everything in me just shook.

"Quiet," the man spoke, his deep voice rumbling the command from beneath my shaking hands.

I muffled my mouth against my fist, willing my heart to slow down.

Somehow, he dropped the older man, who scuttled closer to his legs. The man holding me whipped his phone out, speaking into it, his voice short and curt.

"Perp in the garage. Need you now." Without another word, he hung up and pressed the phone into my chest. "You're safe now; I've got you. Hold this."

I blinked rapidly at him, holding the device in the cradle of my arms. He didn't seem like he was ready to put me down, and I wasn't ready for him to either. I wasn't sure my legs would hold me, and frankly, here, pressed up against him, was the safest I'd felt in a long time.

I couldn't see all of his face from here, only the scruffy edge of his jaw, all dark hair and sharp angles. But I knew what he felt like, my legs still hitched high on his waist as I clung to him.

Solid, warm, and infallible. My thighs clenched slightly as he shifted, and that made his jaw stiffen even more.

"Sorry," I whispered against his shirt.

A warm, strong hand stroked across my lower back, tightening its hold. "It's okay, angel. You're safe now.

"Brooks, what is this?" whispered the older man, who gazed up at us with frank, unhidden fear in his face. I understood that fear. I knew that there was a very real possibility that there was a very dangerous man on the other side of that door. And I wasn't sure whether the giant holding me would be able to hold the door, me, and take care of the guy on the floor all at once.

Brooks—that was his name. I wondered wildly if it was his first or last. I tilted my head, wishing I could look him in the eyes and communicate the throbbing gratitude I felt for him right now. Also wishing very much that I was capable of any sort of speech. My lungs still burned and ached from my drawn-out sprint, and I didn't trust myself to speak and break the moment.

"Joey," my holder said, his voice low. Another similarly outfitted man jogged up the stairs, medium-brown hair tousled as he stepped up to Brooks.

"What's going on?"

Strong arms shifted me, moving me away from the comfort of his body. I almost whimpered. "Can you tell us, angel? Who was that?"

"Was it my wife?" the older man whispered, horror in his voice.

I ignored him, transfixed by the wide, golden-brown eyes that were now looking into mine.

I swallowed twice, digging my fingers into his arms. I had to break his gaze to focus hard on the words. "He's been stalking my friend; he wrote on her car. I didn't know he was still there when I went to check."

The chest under my palms expanded with a sharp breath. "That was very, very dangerous."

"I didn't know," I said, uncalled-for tears welling in my eyes as my adrenaline began to fade.

Two firm fingers slipped under my chin and slowly guided my face up and away. A breath later, I was staring back up into those golden eyes. They really were beautiful. If not for the flutter of thick, black lashes, I'd wonder if there was any way he could be real.

I bit my lip, unsure what he was looking for as he returned my look then swept his stare lower, over what he could see of me from this position. Finally, his face softened, and I felt his hands gentle on where they rested on my waist.

"Go," he muttered to Joey, who was already slipping out into the garage once more. Through the sliver in the door, I desperately looked for any sign of Tiffany.

"My friend..."

"Joey will get her. If she's smart, she ran the other direction." He spoke harshly. "You know you ran to the farthest door, right?"

I flinched away, my stomach clenching at the reproach in his voice. My usually dormant temper welled under my skin, and before I knew it, I was pushing against his arms, my still-quivering legs reaching for the ground.

"You don't have to scold me. I'm not a child. I did what I thought was best." I struggled against the iron bands of his body once more. Putting my elbows to work, I attempted to put distance between myself and this man. I was horrified at the tears still blooming at the back of my eyes. I never cried.

I hated crying. There was no way I was going to blubber all over this Greek God. "Put me down, Mr. Brooks." I took a guess that it was his last name.

"No."

A short, raspy chuckle brought my attention to the man at our feet. "Problems with the halfling, Brooks?"

No? Halfling? My temper bloomed once more, hot under my skin. Did he really just... Wasn't this guy afraid his wife was chasing me in the garage? My thoughts were cut off as the phone in my hands began ringing.

"Pick it up," Brooks commanded, his voice a drawl.

Slowly, I swiped across the screen, staring up at Brooks as I put it close to his ear.

"This is Joey. I have Tiffany. Garage is clear. She's yelling for her friend."

This other man, he had Tiffany. She was safe. We were both safe. Relief made me sag against the muscular chest once again.

Brooks shifted me higher in his arms, with one strong hand suddenly wrapped around my jaw. "Be still, angel. I'm warning you." Something in his voice made me nervous, as if I was made aware that while there may have been a villain chasing me, I was still being held by another stranger. And this one, I felt, may be much, much more dangerous to me.

I needed to take a breath, and there was no way that was happening in this position. "Put me down. Please," I amended at the last moment.

Now that I knew the known danger had passed, I was able to truly take in the deep smirk on his pouty lips. Which made it even more disappointing when they parted to utter a deep, "Or what?"

Ignoring the zing of heat that stole across my belly, I rolled my hips at him, hoping to dislodge his hold on me. More heat flushed through my body as his hand tightened reflexively at my movement.

He was so solid. So strong. So incredibly infuriating.

I put on my best glare. "Keep it up and you'll find out."

Nonchalant, he just kept smirking as we began our to walk to the stairs. "Up, Mr. Salman. The police will be out front. Joey will bring your friend too," he added, looking at me.

I nodded jerkily. "Fine."

To my surprise, the man holding me chuckled, his rumbling voice sending a spike of enjoyment straight up my belly. "Don't sound so grateful."

"I'm sorry. I just—" I replied, trying to sound as strong and sure as I could. Instead, my voice was shaking like a leaf. "Is it really safe? He's really gone?"

"I won't let anyone hurt you," Brooks murmured, his mouth close enough to my ear that I could feel the warmth of his breath. I sighed, his words making my body go boneless against his.

We began the trip back outside the garage, him still carrying me as if I were nothing but a koala curling around his chest. His Mr. Salman mumbled a variety of curse words but followed us as well.

Chapter 2

Asher

Both my brothers would probably pummel the crap out of me if they knew I loved the Chicago Symphony. Over the years, I'd accompanied a few clients to the performances, and it was one of my favorite tourist-feeling things in the city.

Tonight had been no different, and while Mr. Salman had wooed his guests in his private booth, I had soaked in the sweetness of the woodwinds, the violins, and then rest of the orchestra. I couldn't watch much since I had to keep my eyes on Salman, but I was able to listen. And that was enough.

I had not expected how twisted the evening would get when we finally wrapped up in the suite and moved to find Mr. Salman's private car. One moment, I'd been escorting him up a stairway. The next, a tiny dark angel had thrown herself into my arms. She'd been shaking, clinging to me as I tucked all three of us back into the stairs while I hit the emergency button that I wore on my wrist.

Knowing Joey and my brother were alerted to the problem, I'd been able to relax and wait, unsure of what was on the other side of the door. Especially since my mind was consumed with the woman who had attached herself to me. When she'd later asked to be set down, I'd declined, and even I wasn't sure why.

Maybe it was because I was oddly enflamed with anger for how stupid she'd been. Who sees a potential danger and goes walking towards it, barefoot no less? She clearly needed someone to look out of her, and this friend of hers, who now stood by Joey wasn't any good. After all, she'd practically thrown her friend into the fire.

"Are you ever going to put me down?"

I grunted at her question, my chest tight for some reason. "Can you promise me you can walk?"

She glared, and I slipped my everyday mask back over my face, secretly grinning at the spite that flared in her eyes. Stupid she may have acted, but she wasn't lacking in spine. I could admire that all night long.

Well, I guess I could admire all of her, since I wasn't even sure why I was still holding her. But at my core, I was still your basic male. See pretty woman, save pretty woman, hold on to pretty woman. The caveman who lived in the back of my brain was instantly appeased at the perfect curve of her body against mine.

"Brooks... He said your name was Brooks, right?"

I cleared my throat lightly. "Asher Brooks. That's my name."

"And you're his bodyguard?"

"Just temporarily."

Silence fell around us, and I rocked subtly, still savoring the way her lush backside rested so carefully against my hands. It was nearly impossible to not enjoy it. Perks of the job, I reasoned as that plush flesh moved again.

"Did you like the performance?"

I jerked my head down to meet her eyes. "Why do you ask?"

"No reason. Just making small talk."

I snorted and felt her shift as if she smiled. "Thank you," she whispered after a moment. "If you hadn't been there, I'm not sure what I would've done."

"You're welcome," I said curtly, hoping to end this conversation. I was supposed to be watching Mr. Salman, and I could see him growing more and more bored by the proceedings. If I hadn't taken both his keys and his wallet, I would've lost him already.

But that wasn't part of the deal. He could sit his happy butt on the stone wall behind us and wait until I was sure this girl—well, woman—was safe.

The police walked towards us, a tall, willowy blonde—likely Tiffany—by their side. Her tears had dried, but the mascara trails on her face were clear evidence that this had been a horrible night for all of them. And while I was sorry for her stress, it didn't compare to the overwhelming need to keep the girl in my arms safe.

"Lillian, I'm so sorry," Tiffany said, rushing forward. She held her arms out, and slowly, regretfully, I let Lillian slip to the ground. I held tightly to her slender waist as I steadied her. Tiffany's blue eyes flickered briefly to me, questions obvious in her gaze.

Lillian. Feeling my dark angel's name on my tongue, I turned to her friend, allowing the woman to enfold her in a tight hug. I could see Tiffany's mouth drop and whisper frantically into Lillian's ear, all the while giving me a harsh, curious look.

I wasn't sure what she was saying, but I could only imagine.

"Can we go yet?" Salman was whining behind me.

My temper strained at the short leash I kept it on. Turning to my client, I nodded once. "We're done here."

I turned to Lillian, a hundred things bubbling up in my chest, the desire to see her again the strongest urge. But it was "Next time you do something that stupid, just…don't" that slipped off my tongue.

Her jaw dropped, pretty face flushing as she pushed away from her friend to point a finger at me. "How dare you? I thought you were a hero, but you're just a pig."

"It doesn't matter what you think, as long as you are safe." Ah, there it was, the ugly, self-deprecating side of me that savored her change of opinion towards me.

Lillian sputtered, and with a whirl of heavy brown hair, she dismissed me, marching away in measured, careful steps. Her

16

toes were likely torn to shreds, and the muscles in my thighs leapt to retrieve her again, to carry her and protect her from that pain.

But that wasn't my job. I only cared about the people I was paid to do so for.

"It's time to go." I ushered Salman away, my gaze flickering back more than once to the petite figure who clutched her friend's hand, talking animatedly to the police.

She was safe now. Even from me.

***

I scrubbed the bristles of my face as I stared around my apartment. It looked perfect, every surface clean and shining from the maid's latest visit. Not that it mattered. My mother always claimed I'd been an organized kid. As an adult, I thrived in neat environments.

But tonight, even as I slipped into some sweatpants, I found myself distracted. As I perched on the edge of my bed, my mind instantly went back to the woman who had hurled herself at me. She'd felt like heaven against me, even in her moment of fear, which assured me that clearly there had to be something wrong with my head.

It had been too long. I squinted at my phone where it lay across my pillows. How long had it been since I'd indulged in one of the women who lived in my phone to serve exactly that purpose? I didn't do relationships. I'd seen too many torn apart to really be able to trust anyone, or even myself, with another human.

I had my family. My job. My life was fine.

I flopped back on the bed, my legs still dangling off the edge. I didn't need anyone else, so why was I so taken with this literal stranger who had leaped into my arms? Why did I want to see her again? There was some part of me obsessed with the idea of being able to hold her again, to feel the rolling curve of her hips as she settled on top of my body.

With a groan, I took my cock out, letting the semihard erection grow as I ran a finger down the length. Gripping the base, I squeezed, feeling the pumping need filing my body and cock until it ached. Only then did I begin to stroke, using the precum to slick my way up and down the shaft.

I closed my eyes, my head pressing into the pillow as I pictured those puffy bow lips on mine, smiling up at me as I held her against my belly. I wondered how hot she would feel. Would she ride me as sweetly as I imagined?

My hand sped up, tightening as the imagery came together, the way her legs would wrap around me while that smart mouth teased me. It was enough that it sent me over the edge, my cock jerking as stream after stream of cum spread across my belly.

I lay there for a moment, my brain and cock still throbbing. "What a mess," I said to the empty room.

I had no idea what the fascination with this girl meant, but at least I never had to see her again to find out.

***

Lillian

I ran my fingers over the edge of my skirt, tugging at the hemline as I stared around the small, well-furnished office. I couldn't believe I was here. In my entire life, I never guessed that I would have need for personal security. In fact, I found myself rather boring. Even my friends would admit that. My daily life consisted of practicing flute, going for runs around my new apartment in Chicago's bustling downtown, and cuddling with my cat.

But all that was a thing of the past for the time being. Since that night two weeks ago when I'd discovered Tiffany's stalker, things had changed. The man, demented and insane as he must be, had somehow decided to turn his attention to me as well. It started with a simple letter, informing me of my impending doom because I had dared to keep him from his true love.

Yesterday morning, my doorman had mentioned that a man approached him, asking to be let upstairs to my apartment. When he pressed for the necessary information, the stranger had run. Clever enough to evade security cameras, stupid enough to come back. I'd called the policeman who had been assigned to Tiffany's case, and he'd advised me to look for additional help, citing a group called AXE Security.

And now, here I sat, confused and more than a little intimidated.

"I'm sorry you were kept waiting. My lunch meeting ran over," a deep, rolling voice spoke from behind me. I stood quickly, surprised for a moment as I turned to face a version of the infuriating man from the other night in the garage.

I stopped, mentally scolding myself. He—Brooks—had probably saved my life. At minimum, I owed him more than calling him an infuriating asshole mentally.

Especially when I was now staring down someone who had to share at least partial DNA with him. There was no way God was kind enough to make these genetics more accessible, even with the ugly temper.

I wouldn't hold it against him though. We all had that asshole in the family. Shoot, I just did it again. I pasted a smile on my lips, begging my mind to forget about Brooks for five freaking minutes.

"Not a problem. Your assistant was very kind."

"Paula need is the best in the business. It's a miracle she puts up with me at all." He reached a very large hand out, shaking mine gently. "Emerson Brooks. Nice to meet you."

I watched the graceful man make his way around his desk, somehow managing to fold his bulk into a high-backed leather desk chair. "Forgive me for asking, but are you related to..." I trailed off, unsure of where I would go after this question.

Hard amber eyes met mine, a small, polite smile curling his lips. "Yes. My brother, Asher... I believe you may have met him the other night."

I swallowed hard. "I'm very grateful for him." Grateful to and oddly intrigued by. It was a confusing combination.

His brother, older I was guessing, had a very different vibe. This Mr. Brooks exuded a certain type of authoritative tension that reminded me of that time I'd been sent to the principal's office in middle school. I automatically felt like I was in trouble. It was making me fidget.

For a long moment, Emerson Brooks stared at me then seemed to relax, leaning back into his chair. "He's an insufferable ass. I'm sorry for whatever nonsense he spewed at you."

A giggle escaped before I could contain it. "He told me I acted very stupidly the other night." I squirmed in my seat. "And in hindsight, I feel like he was probably right."

Emerson offered a tiny nod. "He is, but don't worry, we don't have to tell him so. Instead, why don't you tell me about what's happening and how we can be of assistance."

As concisely as possible, I explained what had been happening to Tiffany. That a strange person had been leaving letters for her, first at her favorite rehearsal studio, before gaining traction and beginning to address them to her home. Things had escalated, until last week when we'd come out to her car having been spray-painted.

The letter the police found on the concrete around the car, most likely dropped by the perpetrator in his sprint to chase me, had denoted that he wasn't satisfied with being in the background any longer.

Incredibly, the morning after I "saw" him was the first morning that I woke up to a letter of my own, claiming that I had discovered him and that I ruined their chances as a relationship. Tiffany took the first flight out of Chicago back to visit her parents in Kentucky. But me…I had nowhere to go. And I couldn't just upend my life while the police found this creep.

So here I was, hiring my very first bodyguard. It was both completely unbelievable and my only option left.

Emerson listened with rapt, almost sharp intensity. And when I finally ran out of words, and emotion, I sagged in my chair, staring over at him.

"I guess that's all the information I have for you."

"That is more than enough information, Mrs. Oakes."

"It's miss, and I'm glad. I feel like so many people who I've told, or even who Tiffany told, looked at us like we were crazy."

Emerson nodded. "Many people like to discount the impact of stalkers like this. But not us. If you're interested, I say we temporarily station someone with you full-time. After two weeks, we can reevaluate. Does that sound acceptable?"

"I think so. Do you have someone who would be willing to attend my rehearsals with me?" I flushed. "I'm new around here, and I wanted to be sure that I attended as many as I could."

Emerson's smile was kind but gave me the impression he didn't use it often enough. "My people will follow you anywhere, rehearsal or not. But only if it's safe."

I shrugged, unsure of why I even pushed this. "I'd just prefer someone who at least enjoyed or understood music. It's important to me that I don't get distracted by someone who is…bored or even unhappy. It's the musical equivalent of a buzzkill in my mind."

Emerson sat back. "I see what you are saying. I'm sorry I didn't understand the first time." He folded his hands on the desk.

"It's no problem, Mr. Brooks." I stood slowly. "I imagine you will get in touch with me about details?"

"As soon as I have them. You don't have to worry, Miss Oakes. Your safety is our top priority."

Chapter 3

Asher

I was on my second lap around the park adjacent to my neighborhood when I finally stopped ignoring the buzzing in my armband.

Rolling my eyes, I stabbed the answer button and held the phone to my hear, not bothering to stifle the annoyed pant in my voice. "Emerson. God damn, man, what do you want?"

"I have a job for you."

I bared my teeth at my phone, wishing my brother was here so I could thrash him and his three-piece suit. "I told you, I'm not ready to leave the field. I'm happy where I'm at."

"Not the executive job…a field job."

I gripped the phone tightly, breathing through my nose as I attempted to bring my pulse back down to normal. "What's so special about this one?" Usually, my assignments came through either my father or his second-in-command Terry, who handled all distribution of cases. If it was coming from Emerson, it meant one of two things.

One, the job was more important that it seemed on the surface. Or two, my brother was trying to use it to punish me for continuing to ignore his offers to join the management team for AXE Security.

"What is it, then?"

I could feel the carefully veiled command when Emerson answered, "Come in and we can talk about it."

"No." I grinned, enjoying the chance to rebuke my big brother. Too many people ran scared at the sight of him. Someone had to make sure he stayed humble.

"I could make you."

"Could you? Because you're my boss?" I made my voice higher, more irritating.

"No, because you're my shit little brother."

I snorted, humor making my chest swell as I turned towards home. He might be big, bad, and brooding but I still loved the guy. "You could try. You and Xavier have been riding those desks too long. You won't be able to take me down. Even together."

"Mind your words, Asher. You're on speaker."

I chuckled. "Hi, Xavier."

"Prick," my middle brother answered, his voice a low growl. So, they were together. My chest constricted for a short moment, and I stopped to consider the surprising emotion. Was I jealous? Or was it just my stupid youngest child syndrome of constantly feeling left out? Probably that, I reasoned as I marched up the stairs to my doorman.

A long line of women who were perched out on the front patio of the building gave me long, hard looks. To which I replied with a single, heavy wink before I ducked into the cool air of the buildings. I knew they only stared harder, giggling amongst themselves.

"I'll email you all the details. Don't fuck this up."

"Why is this so important?" There was a long pause, in which I poked repeatedly at the elevator button in front of me.

"She's important. Just treat her that way, no matter what."

"That's part of the job, bro. Of course I will."

"I just wanted to hear it from you myself."

I stepped onto the elevator. "In elevator. I'll probably lose you. See you at Mom's for dinner?"

I didn't bother waiting to hear their responses. Of course they would be there. We always attended my mother's infamous end-of-the-month parties. I stepped out onto the top floor, making my way down to my over-large apartment at the end of the hall. Scanning my fingerprint and then my keycode, I slipped inside, wondering to myself whether

Xavier would be bringing his better half, Vanessa, or whether I would be doomed to prodding Emerson into conversation all night.

Vanessa was lovely, far too lovely for any of us Brooks brothers, but I appreciated it all the more. For as much as I ribbed them, I was happy to see my brothers happy. Everyone had something. Emerson had AXE to run, and now Xavier had Vanessa and her rapidly growing belly to focus on.

And I had the job.

Groaning in satisfaction, I stripped off my sweaty shorts and carefully placed them in my laundry basket. The cool water from my shower danced over my skin as I stared blearily at where I'd propped open my phone.

Emerson would've emailed me the case info by now. Why the fuck was I so consumed with this? Something about the way this whole thing had gone down, it crawled under my skin, even now.

"Dammit, Emerson, ruining a perfectly good afternoon off." I snatched the phone off the little shampoo shelf and opened my email, ignoring the droplets of water that blurred my phone screen.

To: Asher.Brooks@AXESecurities.com
From: EmersonBrooks@AXESecurities.com
CC: XavierBrooks@AXESecurities.com
Subject: New Case | Lillian Oakes
Asher,
Don't fuck this up.
Your favorite brother,
E
P.S. Your turn to bring dessert Sunday.

I scrolled past with the wet chuckle. The first file attached was a video file. I open it and turn my volume up, letting the sounds of a woodwind trio fill my shower.

"An artist, eh?" That would be far more enjoyable than listening to financial discussions and quarterly reports. I open the next file, swiping my hand down my face to brush away the lingering shower water.

Lillian Oakes was the filename, and I opened it with gusto, staring as the picture slowly loaded onto my phone. The first thing to appear was a photograph, a young woman with heavy dark curls hanging around a heart-shaped face and serious, deep eyes the color of milk chocolate. Her lips were quirked up on one side, as if she might have considered smiling before settling on this bemused, almost quizzical expression.

I knew her in an instant.

I wanted her even faster.

Lillian Oakes was my dark angel from the garage, brave and stupid and beautiful.

"Fuck you, Emerson," I growled, slamming the file closed. I wasn't a toy to be played with. Not even for this beautiful creature.

Asher Brooks did what he wanted, and I wanted nothing to do with Lillian Oakes.

Well, nothing remotely related to work at least.

Only a sleep later, here I was. I cursed my brothers, my father, God, and St. Michael at each and every step I took as I ascended the steps to Lillian's apartment. It wasn't the height of the inconvenience of a third-story walk-up that I was cursing, but the fact that I was here at all.

I'd tried turning the case down. There were a dozen or more capable agents who would be perfect for Lillian, but Emerson was insistent. Which meant that shortly after I texted him my rejection of the case, my mother had called and told me all about how I should attempt to work with my brothers more often.

When I got off the phone with her, my father had showed up at my door with a bottle of scotch. After a night of cards and too much McClaren, I suddenly found myself here, mere

25

feet away from Lillian's completely ordinary little apartment in the heart of Chicago.

If Emerson was trying to make me quit, he was getting closer and closer to success.

I rapped at the door, tugging down my jacket to straighten the shoulders over my skin. Feeling good, looking good were mutually exclusive, and I wanted this woman to know that whatever had happened last week, I was in charge here.

The door swung open, and standing there in tiny plaid shorts and a white tank top was Lillian Oakes. She was exactly as I remembered...but worse—every inch of her petite, curvaceous body was suddenly exposed to my gaze. I could actually visualize the way my hands would fit around her waist, hoisting her up onto my lap as we clashed together in a fit of need and passion.

"Oh fuck. Of course he sent you," she said, her voice wry and more than a little disappointed. "I should've seen that one coming."

"My brother's sense of humor eludes us all. But..." I stepped forward, into the doorframe, and forced Lillian to take a step back with a squeak that went straight to my cock. I gritted my teeth. "I will complete this mission as requested. Your safety is our utmost importance."

She cocked a hip, drawing my eyes to the smooth flesh at the curve of her ass. I suddenly wished I'd worn my sunglasses inside; those fucking James Bond actors had the right idea.

"I feel like I just heard that exact same thing." She stared up at me, eyes flashing gold. "Well, I don't have time regardless. Get in here. I have to submit this video in a few minutes."

I stepped briskly into her apartment, watching as she moved quickly through a small kitchen space and into the living quarters, where she picked up a long, shining instrument and looked over to me expectantly.

Awkward for the first time in recent memory, I stood in her doorway, watching. What was I supposed to be doing?

"Close the door. My neighbors already hate me enough." Lillian gestures to the flute in her hand, a dry smile on her full lips.

Fighting a blush, I step into the interior of the home and shut the door. I move towards her, pulling my shoulder bag off and place it onto the kitchen counter, removing my iPad. "Do you mean that? Are your neighbors really not fans of you?"

Silence followed, and I glanced up to see literal brown sparks shooting out of eyes as she sat perfectly posed at the edge of a folding chair. In front of her, a laptop was open. Once again, I didn't see the problem.

Suddenly, a slow, accented voice broke the tension between us. "I'm assuming that would be the bodyguard, then?"

Incredibly, Lillian glared harder. I cleared my throat, nodding to her before I slunk away, back towards the door, where I leaned against it, putting as much space between her laptop and me as humanly possible.

I settled into my standard "stare into space" pose, my throat throbbing with the need to scold her, to rip into her about so many things, but to begin with, the fact that she'd already told someone of interest that I was there.

Sometimes a surprise presence was the best way to go. Especially in stalker situations where the solution was to find and remove the threat completely. My hands fisted briefly, thinking about how I'd only been on this case for roughly four minutes and already I'd been thoroughly put into my place.

A soft, vibrating note drew my attention back. Followed by another and another and another. She was playing now, something so sweet and light that it actually made goosebumps erupt all along my arms.

I raised my eyes to her, curious to see what version of Lillian Oakes I might see today. I'd met the angel seeking shelter. I'd seen the devilish tongue. But now, the woman before me was living artwork, her beautiful features schooled and relaxed as her fingers raced up and down the flute's body.

Each note singing out to me as she carefully made her way through this unfamiliar piece.

I was entranced. And confused. Just another side of my new client, which I added to my mental notes.

Minutes later, or perhaps hours, Lillian finally slowed, her graceful hands laying the flute across her lap as she leaned into the screen. She cleared her throat, speaking quietly to whoever was on the other side of the screen.

I couldn't hear it all, nor could I see her lips moving, but as she stood, I heard the last bit.

"Thanks, Phil. I appreciate it. I'll be in touch as soon as this nightmare is over." She tapped a key on the laptop and then stood to pick up her flute case, beginning to wipe down the instrument.

I cleared my throat purposefully.

She shot me a small smile. "He's gone. Feel free to begin scolding me."

"What do you mean?"

"I screwed up, telling him you were here."

I didn't say anything, and she continued. "Your brother, Emerson, left me a whole list of rules, but I just panicked. I'm sorry."

"Who is he?"

Lillian tilted her head as she observed me across the room. "Philip Mattia. My conductor."

I shrug slightly. "He would've had to have been told anyway, as long as you plan to attend regular rehearsals and performances."

My simple words changed everything in the room, the tension evaporating instantly as her lovely face shone with joy. "You're really going to let me do that?"

I moved into the room, watching her close and seal the case. "I'm not your jailer. I'm here to keep you safe. Do you understand the difference?"

Warm sable eyes scanned my face quickly, settling on my lips briefly, and I suddenly wished I could wet them. What was she staring at? I gave in, swiping my tongue across quickly.

"I understand." She stood quickly, her face downcast. "Ready for the tour?"

I nodded, a spike of humor making my chest tighten. I'd already seen the floorplan, of course. And from what I could tell, I would be able to stand in the center of Lillian's apartment and touch every other room, closet, and door without trying.

"You're funny," I said smoothly, following her into her bedroom.

"You think?" She gave me a mocking grin. "Or did you read that in your dossier?"

"Both." I moved into the space, following her and feeling a soft warmth envelope me. There were still a few boxes scattered around the small room, and a pile of laundry sat at the edge of the bed, waiting to be hung. As someone who was obsessively neat, I waited for the irritation to settle in, but instead I found myself enjoying the way she looked there, leaning against the bed and watching me so inquisitively.

Images, bright and vivid, flew behind my eyelids. The way those lips would part when I held her. Those sparkling, emotion-filled eyes that would watch me as I pleasured her. My body stiffened in more than one location, and I shifted, forcing my eyes from her to the small window against the exterior wall.

"Our team was already through here once, but I'll do routine checks until we get settled. I understand you cancelled your plans for the next few weeks."

She nodded. "I just have the one performance, next weekend, that I can't miss. After that, the symphony will be closed for the season."

I nodded. I knew that, but for some reason I lingered, letting her explain.

"So, it's just you and me, here...for the next two weeks?" I glanced over at her, my lips curving as I note the soft blush in her cheeks. Maybe I wasn't the only one being struck by the intimacy of this moment.

"Just you and me." I stepped towards her, enjoying the twang of pleasure that took hold of me, pulling tighter and tighter as I stopped directly in front of her.

"Does that make you nervous, angel?"

Chapter 4

Asher

She blinked rapidly, her mouth opening and closing for a moment. Then with a shake of her head, she attempted to move past me. One tiny bare foot caught on the edge of a box, and she twisted, gravity tugging her to the ground. I spun, my hands finding holds on her forearm and around the curve of her waist.

I heaved her away from the hardwood floors, pulling her directly to my body. She was panting, surprise making her pretty lips pop open as she stared straight up into my face.

"I've got you," I grunted, feeling the way her soft body stilled against mine. Just as it did the other night, as if again, she instinctively understood the safety I offered.

"Oh," she murmured. Her eyes were doing that thing again, the golden flecks glowing as she focused in on me. "Thank you."

"You're welcome."

She swallowed and for some reason I couldn't stop watching the line of her throat as it moved. Landing on the space where her pulse fluttered. I could press a kiss there, feel that rush under my tongue.

"You can let me go now," she whispered, voice shaky.

I dropped my face closer, ignoring every warning in my mind as I grew closer, letting the smell of her fill my nostrils. "Of course. My apologies." I stepped away quickly, straightening and taking a very large step away from her.

My hands burned with awareness of how good she'd felt. I needed to be more careful. I wasn't going to ruin a fifteen-year streak of focused security because some sexy flutist felt like sin against my body. Flautist? Flute player. Whatever she was, she was only a client.

"Excuse me. I need to make a phone call." I instilled as much ice into my words as possible, and I could see the immediate change on Lillian's face. She nodded, but her expression was subdued.

"I'm going to shower and get ready for a day of sitting around the house." Her words stuttered out at the end statement, but the dismissal was clear either way.

I nodded and moved back out to the living area and found a bar stool to perch on at her breakfast bar.

As soon as I heard the water turn on, I whipped out my phone.

Asher: I don't think I can stay on this job.
Emerson: In love already?
Asher: Fuck you.
Emerson: So that's a yes. You're welcome.
Asher: Again, fuck you. What's your angle?
Emerson: No angle. Just work.
Asher: Liar.
Emerson: Do your job, Asher.
Asher: I'm telling Mom.

After five minutes, I contented myself with scrolling through my email. My brother wasn't responding, and I didn't dare call him on the phone. I may match Emerson in sheer size and athletic prowess, but I couldn't hold a candle against him in a negotiation skills.

I was staying here, with Lillian Oakes, for the next two weeks. There was no getting out of it.

Time to go to work.

***

Lillian

I was twenty-three. I'd been supporting myself since I graduated college. I wasn't broke, but it wasn't like I was rolling in money.

One thing I splurged on was nice bath towels. There was nothing like stepping out of a steamy shower and straight into soft, dry comfort.

They were also handy on days like this, where I was currently curled up on my bathroom floor, hands over my eyes as I tried to talk myself out of storming back out into my living room and demanding Asher Brooks get the heck out of my apartment.

Or asking him to kiss me. Depending upon the moment, I was varying wildly between those two options. The kiss, definitely tempting. But the man, absolutely infuriating. I shifted on the cool tile, wrapping my towel around my legs. I guess if I was kissing him, he wouldn't have the ability to say anything stupid. That was a definite perk and a vote for the kiss theory.

But first, a shower. I piled my hair onto my head, wrapping a scrunchy around my thick bun before stepping into the searing water. I let the water wash over me, cleansing away the anxieties of the day, the strange memories of my practice session, and finally the way I could almost feel the exact location of each of Asher's fingers when he'd caught me just a few minutes ago.

I sighed, gripping my favorite lavender soap and rubbing it across my skin. Under my flesh, my body hummed with barely repressed excitement. There was no lying there. My body wanted him. My body didn't care that he talked to me like I was a child. My body only cared that he was six foot five and filled out that suit like he was born with it on.

Could I imagine what he looked like with it off? You bet I could.

Oh my God. I actually dropped the soap as I realized for the first time that Asher was staying with me long term, as in for the next fourteen days, and in my one-bedroom, one-bath apartment.

I glanced around my narrow shower. Would he even fit in here? He definitely wouldn't fit in with me. Heat unrelated to the shower flooded my body. Why was I thinking like that?

Maybe it was just my way of dealing with the fact that I was about to live with a man for the first time in my life. And he was ridiculously beautiful.

I pressed my knees together. God help me be strong.

***

I sliced through a cucumber, tossing it into a bowl of waiting vegetables for a simple salad to go with my dinner tonight. Asher seemed to be watching keenly, his dark eyes curious as I put together my meal.

"Will you be joining me?"

"For dinner? No, I prefer to eat later."

"How will you do that? With the…situation?" I bit my tongue, begging myself to stop talking. I had just called myself a situation. This man had be rattled.

A ghost of a smile pulled at his lips. "Are you worried about me?"

I ducked my head, confused at how to respond to this soft flirt after his cold, strange attitude earlier. I gripped the homemade dressing I'd just made, dripping it over my vegetables and tossing it lightly.

"I brought over several meals for myself. They're tucked into your fridge."

I nodded, focusing my attention on the food in front of me.

"I was surprised at how full your fridge was. Do you like to cook?"

I smiled, pleasure at his interest making my belly quiver. "I do love to cook. It's my way to relax."

"I can tell."

"If you change your mind and want to eat with me, you are welcome to it." I jerk an elbow at the remaining leftovers as I made a plate for myself and carried it over to the sofa. Most nights I sat on the barstool where Asher currently sat, but there's no way I could trust myself to sit next to him right now. Not with all this pent-up…frustration lurking around.

As soon as my ass hit the cushion, I flipped on a favorite true crime investigation show and settled in. A second later, the couch dipped again, and I looked over to find Asher sitting right next to me.

I took a long bite, crunching through my greens as I contemplated how the next two weeks was going to look. Swallowing forcibly, I examined at him under my lashes. Only to find him staring right back.

I coughed a little, my vinaigrette suddenly a bit spicier than I'd intended it. I felt my nose and eyes begin to run as I struggled to swallow down the surprise. Asher's hand landed on my shoulder blades, pressing gently.

I cleared my throat, looking up at him through bleary eyes. His broad hand slipped from my back as his thumb slowly brushed away the tear that escaped from one eye.

"Are you alright?"

I nodded, coughing one more time before I sagged into the couch.

"It'd be rather embarrassing if my client choked on salad dressing under my watch."

I chuckled weakly. "Off to a great start, aren't we?"

Something in his eyes changed as he looks me over. I felt nearly naked in my sweatpants and T-shirt. "I think so."

I tilted my chin up, staring at him once more. That icy exterior was gone again for the moment, the hungry, intense Asher showing through as he trailed his thumb down my cheek, taking my rogue tear with him.

I quickly looked down at my dinner. If I was nervous before, now I was freaking terrified. And not because of my spicy dressing. Because the man right next to me was looking more and more kissable by the moment.

It was going to be a long two weeks.

***

I was wrong. It was a very, very long four days. That was exactly how long it had been since Asher came catapulting in my life. There had been a lot of very good things. For instance, I'd discovered he was incredibly easy to live with. He was neat, polite, picked up after himself, and didn't steal the remote.

I'd known that hiring a bodyguard would be drastic, but actually having another human exist as your shadow was definitely something I had to get used to. It didn't hurt that when he posted up by the door or sat at the barstool working on his laptop, he might as well as have been beautiful, living art.

And then there was what he liked to do in the mornings, which had me reaching for my phone to text Tiffany as I lay in bed, listening to the sounds coming from my living room.

Lillian: OMG. He's working out again.
Tiffany: You know what that means.
Lillian: I can't believe I told you that.
Tiffany: You are a good friend who took pity on me stuck here with my parents while you are squashed into nine hundred square feet with a man who makes Greek Gods look like playthings.
Tiffany: What are you wearing?
Lillian: Blue nightgown, Target.
Tiffany: Underwear?
Lillian: Yes? Why is that a question?
Tiffany: Just curious how fast you want to move this along. You only have ten more days.
Lillian: Tiff!
Tiffany: Someone's got to get some, and you are in a way better position than me.
Lillian: This conversation is over.
Tiffany: Has he come in to shower yet?
Lillian: NO.

Tiffany: Good. Take a picture.

A knock at the door made me squeak and throw my comforter back over my legs as I hid my phone under the covers with me.

"Lillian, are you up?" Asher's voice was deep and rumbling through the door.

My toes clenched under the blanket as my hand gripped my phone, as if he might somehow know what I'd just been talking about.

I blamed the lack of interaction, but right now, seeing Asher come marching into my bedroom in the mornings was the best part of the entire day. I didn't have much to look forward to, so I'd made it a bit of a habit to stay in bed later, hoping to catch him.

"Come on in," I called lightly, trying to sound less guilty.

My knob turned, and in a breath, Asher Brooks filled my doorway once more, except this time it was the entry to my bedroom. I'd love to say that I'd gotten used to this little ritual of his, but I hadn't. He worked out in the wee hours of the morning, his soft grunts and the sounds of his body as he moved around the living room waking me up every day.

And then…God help me, he came through my room to shower. He always brought his clothes with him, usually a nice button-down and dress pants, so it wasn't like he walked around in a towel, but at this point, I wouldn't be so upset with it.

Because from what I could see of Asher in his shorts and tank top, I would like to climb him like a tree.

Just like each of the previous mornings, Asher gave me that professional nod and moved into the bathroom. "Good morning," he tossed over his shoulder as he meandered across the space.

I smiled at him, unworried about him seeing me in my pajamas by this point.

Just as he turned, I scrambled, whipping out my phone, and before I could second-guess myself, I snapped a photo of the broad back of his shoulders, the narrow, lean hips, and long legs that peaked out of his mid-thigh-length shorts.

As if sure of what I'd just done, Asher turned slightly, his eyes hot on me. His grin was pure sex. "Make sure to get my good side."

My blush was so expansive I thought for sure I was going to combust. I flopped back, covering my face with my arms as deep, attractive laughter sounded from inside my bathroom.

Tiffany owed me big-time.

With a bitter grunt, I sent the picture off to my best friend before preparing to hide under the covers again.

After a minute, I heard a tentative knock at the front door.

I bolted upright. I hadn't been expecting anyone, but there was a tight-knit community in my building. I wouldn't be totally surprised to find a neighbor coming by to say hello or check in. I had basically turned into a hermit in the past few days. I swung my legs to the ground and grabbed my robe from the foot of the bed.

Asher had already showed me how to work his system of small, easy hidden cameras. He had them stashed everywhere around the apartment and the building. Poking a few buttons, I opened up the window into a video stream of the apartment hallway. It was a shorter guy, his blond hair in a crew cut and wearing a plaid shirt. I recognized him as my neighbor from down the hall.

Chris? I think that was his name. He seemed harmless enough, and I'd clearly known him far longer than the stalker had shown up. Tightening the sash on my fluffy robe, I moved into the other room, heading straight to the door and unlocking the various locks there.

"Hi," Maybe Chris said, a bright smile on his face. He was rather cute, and suddenly I felt self-conscious of my appearance. I pulled the robe a little tighter.

"Good morning," I said softly, keeping the door only open about a foot. "Is everything okay?"

"I just noticed you hadn't picked up your mail or packages and wanted to check on you. Are you sick?" Chris offered me a kind look.

I gave him a small smile. "Oh, that's so nice of you. But no, just been so busy with work, and it must've slipped my mind."

"I could bring them to you if you'd like?"

A deep, rough voice answered for me. "Lillian, why don't you introduce me to your friend?"

I could feel the wet heat of Asher standing behind me. And as I turned, the door widened, showing every inch of Asher Brooks as he stood behind me in only a towel. I stared. Chris stared. A dangerous drop of water dared to blaze a path down the center of Asher's chest, as if to draw even more attention to the smooth play of muscles under the dusting of dark hair.

I took in a sharp breath.

"Chris, this is Asher. Asher, this is my neighbor, Chris."

Chris stared, wide-eyed and shocked, as he took in the picture we made together. Somehow, he pulled himself together enough to nod at the other man, his hands slipping into his pants pockets.

"Lovely to meet you. Did you need something?" Asher ran a frustratingly large hand through his still-wet hair, now hanging dark and long to his ears.

"Um, no, sorry man... I..." Chris looked between us, as if waiting for me to bail him out. But Asher didn't give him the chance.

His lips curled into a dark smile as he stared down at the smaller man. "As you might imagine, Lillian and I have a few things that we should get back to." He slipped a finger into the back of my robe and pulled me flush to his body, a possessive hand slipping around my shoulders, where he caressed my collarbone.

"I should go."

"Goodbye, Chris," Asher said, a note of sarcasm ringing true.

"Bye, Chris. Thanks for checking—" My words were cut off as Asher dragged me back into the apartment and shut the door forcibly.

There was a long, heavy moment as Asher and I stared at each other, and then he stepped into my space, pushing me back against the heavy door, his bare arms caging me in.

"What the hell were you thinking?"

"He's my neighbor."

"He could be dangerous."

I almost rolled my eyes. "He's not."

"He is."

I opened my mouth, and Asher raised a finger, jabbing it in my face, his own expression thunderous. "He is. Every man is when it comes to you. I would do anything, and I mean anything, to keep you safe. But you have to trust me."

I was breathing hard now, staring up into Asher's face as my entire body bowed up to his, as if seeking his reassurance even now.

His eyes dropped to my mouth. Arousal pooled between my thighs, making my skin hot.

"Do you trust me, Lillian? Tell me."

"I trust you."

Asher leaned in, his huge body molding over mine as every one of my senses was consumed with him. "Good girl," he whispered, his voice rough against my skin.

"I won't do it again."

"I know you won't." Asher slowly pushed back, peeling his body away from mine as he turned and moved back towards the bathroom and his clothing.

As he did, I realized just how honest I'd been. I did trust Asher Brooks with my life. Maybe even with my body. But I knew I could never trust him with my heart.

That was off-limits.

Chapter 5

Asher

I hadn't taken a warm shower since I'd started this case. Every morning, I woke up, did as much of a workout as I could in her tight little living room, and then strolled through her bedroom to take a shower in her bathroom.

I'd been spoiled apparently. Most people who could afford our services were incredibly well off financially and threw me into one of their spare bedrooms—or even rented adjourning rooms. And I'd never wished more for that in my whole life.

Because Lillian Oakes was intoxicating. Other than our random scuffles, like when she'd opened the front door in her god-damned robe, I found myself enjoying being around her.

She loved to read, played her flute for hours a day, and spent any spare time she had watching action hero movies.

It if were any other situation, I'd be falling all over myself to get her attention. But in this case, I had her attention for the wrong reasons. She was my client, and I was a professional.

Besides, women like her married up in the world. There was no way she would ever dirty her hands with a boujee version of a gun for hire. That or a babysitter, depending on the client.

We were two different people with very different futures, and I could respect that. While I'd been tempted to ask her to share my bed...or in this case, her bed, something about using her just for pleasure, not starting something long-term, didn't sit well. If I ever had the chance with someone like Lillian Oakes, I would make sure she never got away again.

Maybe that was why at thirty-five, I was realizing that I had been enjoying my cool, lonely apartment less than I had been telling myself.

"Asher?" A soft voice snapped me back to the present, where Lillian stood in her small horseshoe-shaped kitchen, spatula in hand. I could tell she'd already said it a few times based on her curious expression.

"I'm sorry. What did you say?" I stood, unfolding myself from my side of her sofa and moving to her. I hadn't put on my jacket in a while, preferring to stay in my dress shirt and trousers on the days the two of us were stuck inside together.

Lillian's eyelashes fluttered as I came closer, and I could see the way her body stiffened. Whether it was in interest or nerves, I still wasn't sure.

"I was just wondering if you wanted any breakfast. I made too many eggs."

My stomach threatened a growl, which I clenched my belly over, attempting to muffle the sound. I had a perfectly good protein bar sitting inside the container I'd stowed away on top of her refrigerator. But the idea of actually eating that now was less than exciting.

"I'd love some." The truth flowed easily.

Lillian did a double take, which made my lips quiver. "Really?"

"Really." I sat in one of two barstools, making sure that there was plenty of room, and invited Lillian to join me on the second. She'd been nervous around me at first. Putting as much space as possible between us. So when she did, I couldn't stop the contented warmth that spread across my chest and down my fingers.

The eggs were soft, slightly salty, and so much more enjoyable than my breakfast bar. Maybe I should let her feed me more often.

"Who taught you to cook?"

Lillian smiled. "It was born out of necessity. My parents worked late, and I've always had an interest in food. As soon as I could figure out the stovetop, I started helping cook our dinners." She twirled her fork in the air. "I always told my parents that I wanted a dozen kids. They thought I was kidding, but I want to have huge family dinners. I want to pile in around the TV to watch movies. Being an only child is great, but it's quite lonely."

"You would love my family. My brothers are...well, you've met Emerson. But don't hold that against us. My parents are lovely and far more emotionally available than us."

Lillian giggled. "I wasn't going to say anything."

"You don't need to. We know what we are like."

She took a bite of her eggs, and I stared at the soft pink of her tongue as she licked her lips. "Why is that, then?"

"I guess in my case, no woman has ever expressed much interest in me." The truth was heavy in the air. "Other than the obvious."

"Oh yeah, it's obvious, then?"

I tilted my head, a bit confused. "I guess it was to me. Women only want something simple from me, something temporary."

"And you don't? No offense meant, Asher, but you come off like a..."

I took another bit of eggs, swiveling my chair to face her. I smiled, but it felt fake on my lips. "Say it."

"Kind of a man whore," Lillian blurted out, covering her mouth immediately afterwards. "God, I'm so sorry, Asher. That's not how I see you at all."

"And why not? If everyone else thinks that, why don't you?"

Lillian's fingers, long and delicate, slowly peeled away from her face. "Because I see you. I've seen you every day this week, and I can tell how much you want to take care of people."

"I get *paid* to take care of people."

"Not like that. I can see you listening to the music, and I heard you calling your mother the other night. You might look like some kind of playboy, but I think you have a good heart. That should be what's important."

I stared at her hard, half afraid she was moments from bursting into laughter. But she remained still, a patient smile on her exquisite lips.

"Thank you, angel." The pet name slipped out before I could stop myself. For a long, drawn-out moment, I thought she might get mad.

But to my surprise, an adorable blush colored her cheeks. "I've never had a nickname before, but I really like that one."

My throat constricted, thankfully saving me from the confession that I had never given another woman a nickname like that. But as with everything else Lillian, I was off my game and getting too close.

I cleared my throat, pushing my half-eaten plate back to her. "I have to step out to meet with the rest of the team for tonight. Promise me you'll stay here and out of trouble."

"Will do. I've got plenty to do before the concert."

I wasn't sure if she was being entirely truthful, but I couldn't dwell on that right now. I had a team to prep and a woman to protect. Gritting my teeth, I made myself walk away from her.

She was the most important thing in my life right now, and I was going to do what I had to do to protect her.

***

I stayed away for as long as I could without slacking on my job. I even came back and stationed myself outside her apartment in the building's interior hallways for a while. Anything to remind myself that this was a job. Lillian was not mine, not really. She was mine to protect, and after the end of next week, we would be done.

I'd probably never see her again.

I probably *shouldn't* ever see her again.

I glanced at my phone, briefly debating on whether I should respond back to my mother's chain messages about attending a cousin's wedding in a few weeks. Since I had neither an answer or any interest in listening to her remind us of all that she was getting older and desperately wanted to have more grandbabies as soon as possible, I left it on unread.

A soft knock sounded on the door behind me, and I turned to observe it. Had Lillian just knocked on the interior of her apartment? As if she were asking permission to enter the hall?

I smothered a chuckle and reached down to scan the recently upgraded thumbprint doorknob and waited until it beeped and the door swung open. All laughter died in my chest as I stared down into Lillian's warm brown eyes. She was dressed in a curve-hugging black cocktail dress with soft fluttering sleeves and a generous V-neck design.

With our height difference and the dress's kindness, I was treated to an unaltered view straight down her top, where I could see just the edge of her black lace bra and the generous swell of her breasts. They really were perfect; she should show them off. I knew in an instant they'd fit perfectly into my hands, the softness of her body pulling me in like a fly to honey.

"Lillian," I finally forced out, my eyes sweeping lower to soak in every inch of her.

"I just called for my ride. I assume you want to join us?"

"Cancel it. I will drive us."

"What? Really?"

Yes, because I wasn't ready to let anyone else see her like this. Some inexplicable need washed over me to come up with a reason to keep her home tonight. More couch and TV. More card games. More of only me being able to watch over her.

I stamped down on the urge to say any of those things or go completely crazy and swing her over my shoulders and carry her back inside.

I nodded.

Her smile was bright, excitement over the outing shining out at me, making me feel like even more of the garbage human I was. I couldn't keep her here. She had a job to do, just like I did. And I would be sure that she was safe while she did it.

"I'm going to change my shirt; do I have a minute?"

Lillian nodded, moving to allow me to come back inside. Typically, I changed in the bathroom or, when she was in her bedroom, quickly in the living room. But something had changed, and I wanted her eyes on me.

I wanted her attention.

I slipped my jacket from my shoulders, tugging at my tie as I did. I heard the soft patter of her feet as she moved into the kitchen, trapped between her bedroom and me. She could turn around, but I knew she wouldn't. I'd felt her eyes on me all week, and now I savored it. I needed to capture it and hold it tight tonight as I was forced to share her with the world.

Button by button, my shirt opened, and I subconsciously flexed my abdominal muscles. I heard the quiet catch in her voice as I tossed the dirty shirt at my suitcase and kneeled to thumb through the carefully laid out replacement.

When I stood and turned back to her, she'd moved, coming to stand directly in front of me.

"Lillian?" My voice was deep, raspy as I realized how close she was. I could feel her breath as she stared up at my bare chest. I watched as the edge of her tongue slipped out to wet her lips.

"What are you trying to do?"

"I'm not sure what you mean?" I move to thrust my hands into my sleeves, but she stopped me with a brush of her fingers down my chest.

"Every time I think I've figured out you, you change again. One minute, so cold. The next..." She ran her fingers carefully over my ribs to rest right over my belly button. "So hot."

I swallowed, unsure of how to answer her. Because what she said wasn't just the truth, but it was the definition of my life. I stayed cold to protect my job. But with her, it was all messed up, blended together.

I gritted my teeth, my balls aching as I felt her fingertips trace a line in my skin. "You change things."

"Like what?" Her voice was soft, like the rest of her. And innocent.

I shuddered. "You make me want to be...better."

She smiled at that, lipstick-stained lips curling into a perfect bow. I want to throw her down on my makeshift bed and smear that lipstick right off. My cock jumped in my pants, a heavy throb responding in my chest as I stepped even closer, pushing against her hand.

It flattened, holding me carefully away.

"You don't need to be better, you know. You just need to be you."

A soft vibrating noise broke the heat between us.

"That's my phone," I told her quietly. "The team must be getting into place. Are you ready?"

Lillian's chest expanded as, slowly, she pulled her hand away. Her eyes flashed to mine. "For what it's worth, I don't think you needed to be better. I think you just needed to be given a chance."

My heart stumbled to a halt as she moved around the room, gathering her things. Was she right? Maybe I'd always just been waiting for the right moment. And maybe I'd just found it.

Chapter 6

Lillian

I didn't even make it into the building.

Asher did. About six inches before his head flew up, hand going to his headset and then his phone. It only took me another second or two to recognize the look on his face. Something had gone wrong.

"How did he get in?"

In? My stomach dropped, making my throat tight and achy as I watched Asher's face change.

Suddenly, sharp, angry cries sounded from within the performance center's backstage area.

"What is that?"

Asher's body covered mine, his words blurring as colorful smoke filled the hallway we were headed into.

"Shit." Asher's jaw was clenched and angry. "He spray painted stupid crap all over the floors and walls of the stage. Left little smoke bombs down the hall."

I grimaced, knowing how many angry people were in there blaming me. "Why would he do that?"

Asher went completely still. "He wants you to go home."

Something clicked in my brain, making my heart stammer. "Do you really think so? Would he do something like that?"

"It doesn't matter. I'm not taking any risks when it comes to you."

***

Asher

Every moment of training, every second I'd spent protecting other people. It had all come down to this moment so that I could be here with Lillian, protecting her from whatever this nameless evil was.

I moved through the rapidly exiting crowd, Lillian's slender body locked to mine as I used my bulk to shield her from anyone between us. I'd studied these streets religiously; I knew at least four different ways to get out of the area.

I shifted my watch, the button on my electronic face blinking. I'd hit it as soon as I'd heard the sound change in the main hall. I'd expected something, but not something so public, such a spectacle. I hope this asshole made himself enough of one that the police would easily be able to figure out who he was.

For Lillian's sake.

"Asher, please, my feet," Lillian stuttered, her body bowing over as she attempted to yank her heels off her feet.

"We have to go," I growled at her, swinging my arms low to wrap around her body and toss her and her goddamned shoes over my shoulder. We had no time to stop, not an instant to hesitate as long as Lillian was in danger.

"Asher," she whimpered as I hurried down a small staircase and into the final parking lot. I was suddenly furious with myself that I hadn't let her hire a driver.

"Almost there. Stay with me." I pressed a hand to the back of her thigh, feeling the cold, smooth flesh there and holding tight to her. I could practically feel her fear as we turned the final corner to my assigned AXE vehicle.

I slowed, dropping my shoulder so she could slide to the ground. One more movement, and I practically shoved her into the large SUV. I moved around to the driver's side, straightening my suit as I went. It was an act, this pretend calm, but one I savored. There was power in it, acting so calm in the face of danger.

I typically savored these moments, my ego inflating like some kind of cock-shaped balloon. But now, there was real pressure in my body, begging me to hurry and run to the driver's seat of the vehicle. To get her away from here.

I got into the SUV, pressed the car to life, and pulled out onto the frontage road. My phone went to my ear, even as I smiled at Lillian, gesturing at her seat belt.

Slowly, fingers shaking, she pulled at the shoulder strap, her body trembling so much that it took several tries before she could pull it across her body.

"Emerson," I said into the phone. "We've got a problem. They were able to bypass concert security as well as Antonio's setup."

"You need to move her. Do you have a plan?"

A plan? Of course, I had a plan. I was going to take the woman beside me and whisk her far away from this danger, and then I was going to build a wall around the two of us and spend the rest of my day ravishing her and quelling any and all of her fears. Once that was done, I was going to hunt down the bastard who was taking so much pleasure in scaring her and make him pay.

Then maybe more ravishing.

I gritted my teeth, using my shoulder to hold my phone as I leaned over and pushed the buckle of Lillian's seat belt more firmly into the lock. She sent me a grateful look, and incredibly, she reached across the console to set her hand on my leg.

Her face was pale, her brown eyes wide, but she was gazing at me with complete and utter trust. It filled me with intention.

"I do. I have a plan," The solution, insane as it would've seemed a few weeks ago, now satisfied me to no end. "We'll be at the penthouse."

Emerson was silent for a moment before speaking. "You know what you're doing. Let me deal with the police. Update me in the morning."

"Done."

"Hey, Asher," Emerson said, his voice practically a whisper.

"Yeah?" I took a sharp right turn, putting us on the path to my home.

"Take care of yourself. And her."

My foot hesitated on the gas, almost slowing my ascent up the ramp. Emerson didn't say things like that. At least not usually. I chuckled a little into the phone.

"Don't get soft on me now, big brother."

Emerson hung up, and it made me smile. That was more like it.

I tossed the phone into my cupholder and captured the delicate, shaking hand that was still pressed against my thigh.

"Asher..." Her voice was shaking almost as much as she was. "What's going to happen now?"

"I'm going to keep you safe. Just like I promised." I didn't bother trying to stop myself from gripping her fingers and pulling her hand to my lips. I pressed a kiss there, feeling the soft, cool skin.

I could feel the shuddering sigh she let out, and I wasn't sure whether I'd helped or hurt the situation. But I pressed another kiss there because I couldn't stop myself. Feeling her flesh against mine was more soothing than anything else could be at this moment.

She was safe.

I had her.

I was taking her home so that I could protect her even better than before.

The drive was filled with silence after that. I held her hand in mine, settling our entwined fingers on the console as we mad our way over to my building. Private parking, coded garage entry, and multiple fingerprint doorways soothed my anxieties.

This was my domain. This was where she belonged.

With her heels dangling from her fingertips and me shepherding her through my private entrance, we made it upstairs with no issues. Surprising, since every beat of my heart was screaming for me to pick her up again. To cradle her close and make sure that no one ever had any doubts who had her.

She is mine, my ridiculous brain screamed.

I hurried her down the hall to my door, and after a variety of beeps, the door swung open. Lillian allowed me to gently press her inside, the darkness swallowing us as I shut the door again.

In the dark, I could feel the delicate hand as it pressed against my chest. Questioning and uncertain.

"Why did you bring me here?"

My chest was heaving, every part of my body so singularly focused on her that I was surprised she couldn't feel it. But then I heard her gasp softly. She did feel it.

I heard her shoes tumble to my floor she pressed her hand against my jawline, fingertips searching me out. My control snapped like the breaking of a dam, and I was on her in an instant. My arms swept around her waist to lift and guide her around my torso. My hands ran up and down her spine, feeling the delicate little protrusions of her bones as I stumbled forward, pressing her against the wall in my entryway.

"Never again," I growled, my mouth hovering over hers. My hands dropped lower and gripped the softness of her backside. "Never."

Her breath washed over my face as she spoke again, and I suck it into my body, desperate for any taste of her I could get. "Never what?"

"I will never let you put yourself as risk again. You will stay here, safe, with me, until they find him." I ran my nose up and down the side of her face, the now-familiar smell of her soap teasing my senses.

She slipped her arms around my neck and tightened her hold on me. "You want me to stay here."

Yes, of course I did. "I demand it."

Her breath caught, and then she pressed back. "Don't I get a choice?"

I gripped her ass tighter, leaning my body over hers so she could feel not only our size difference, but the difference in control. As in, I was barely holding back from ripping her panties down her legs and slamming into her right there in the hall.

She would do what I said, because that's what would keep her safe.

From him.

She moved against me, curious and shivering. I groaned, feeling the way the heat of her core pressed against my belly. I was so close; my cock was aching in my pants, and all I could think about was how far I would have to make it into my apartment before I could find a more suitable surface to take her on.

Her lips pressed against my neck, and my knees almost gave. "You always have a choice. But please..." I, Asher Brooks, pleaded with my sweet, shy little client, "let me protect you."

She pressed another kiss to where my pulse was fit to bursting in my neck. "I know you won't let anything hurt me."

Hurt her.

Fuck.

I stepped back so fast that she actually squealed a little and tightened her hold once more. I clenched my eyes shut, even in the dark, reaching for depth of control I'd never had to use before.

Because I'd been moments from taking her. Maybe minutes, if she'd been lucky enough that I would've lasted long enough to make it into my bedroom.

And after next week, I would never see her again. She was part of my job. She'd humored me, even been attracted to me, but she would want more.

She wanted a forever love. And I was a *for tonight* fuck.

I would break her heart. Right after I broke her headboard.

"That's the job," I finally said, relaxing my hands and letting her slip to the floor. Every brush of her body against mine was torture as I slowly reeled in my emotions, stuffing them behind my favorite smirking, cool mask of indifference.

It was a lie of course. But it was a lie I had to stand behind. For her. For her safety.

"Your room is over here. You should go get cleaned up. I have to speak with Emerson and the officials."

I didn't need the light above my head to see the confusion and hurt that I unleashed on her already quaking heart with my words.

I was an asshole.

I stepped forward, landing a heavy hand on her shoulders to guide her through the foyer and to where I could flip on the lights. After I did, it was obvious which room was hers—the small guest room opening right to my high ceilings and sprawling living space.

Lillian didn't look at me. She simply turned to the room, her bare feet making no noise against the plush carpet.

"Lillian," I stammered, miserable.

She doesn't respond, but her steps slowed, and she turned to look over her shoulder at me, allowing me to see one dark, tear-filled brown eye.

"I'm trying to protect you."

She tilted her head, eyes narrowing as she observed me and my words. "Are you?" She stepped towards the bedroom, her black cocktail dress still wrinkled by my hands. She stopped in the doorway to her new room, waiting until the door was half closed before flicking her gaze back up to me. "Or are you protecting yourself?"

She shut the door, leaving me standing outside of it, aching, hard, and with a distinctive pain in my chest. One I hadn't felt for a very long time.

Fuck me.

Chapter 7

Lillian

I was going to need enormous amounts of therapy. There was no doubt about that. And it wasn't just because I had a mega-creep stalking my best friend and me.

It was because of Asher Brooks.

That man had been building me up for weeks. The casual, slow looks he gave me that fed my self-esteem. The sweet touches when he thought I might mistake them for a casual "we live in a tiny apartment together and it can't be avoided."

But I knew the truth behind the smirk. Asher Brooks wanted me.

And it freaking terrified him.

Me on the other hand? I was no different. Terrified didn't cover it one bit, but it was for a very different reason. Whatever vision he might have for having sex with me, I was bound to ruin it. I was a freaking twenty-three-year-old who'd had sex only one time in her whole life. And it was prom night.

I was a walking 90s movie plot line. And he—well, shit, Asher was walking sex. Everything he did made my mind reel and my thighs clench. I loved to spar with him, I loved to cook for him, and I loved the way he studied me when he didn't think I was paying attention.

For a bodyguard, he was pretty unaware really. Because I wanted him too. Tonight, for just a moment, I thought I'd gotten through to him.

But I was wrong. Asher would never see me as anything other than a short-term project, a client he'd enjoyed flirting with. It only disappointed me further when tonight he'd claimed that by pushing me away, he was actually protecting me again.

How on earth did you convince someone that while they were so obsessed with being bad at relationships, they actually were actually the very best? And, in my case, the only one I wanted?

I needed an idea on how to convince him I could take care of myself, at least in regard to him and his intensity.

He would be an amazing partner. And I could feel the way he would care of me. A sharp tingle wound its way through my body and ended in the dark heat between my legs. He would be an amazing father. That tingle grew, and I fidgeted under the covers.

I eyed the door. It was closed, but of course there was no lock, as it was probably never intended to be used as an actual guest room. Since, as Asher had explained one lunch while he pretended to not enjoy my cooking, he didn't invite friends over. And never, ever had clients here.

Yet here I was. Alone, stressed, and more than a little horny from our most recent clash of opinions.

Biting my lips, I let my fingers slip under the T-shirt I'd found in one of the drawers. It was a plain gray color and soft enough that I had immediately exchanged my cocktail attire for it before slipping into bed.

My skin hummed, adrenaline still spiking in my blood and urging me on as I drew my thumbs over my nipples and then down each of my ribs slowly, feeling the gooseflesh that rose as I did.

I'd given up on my panties, throwing them over in the chair with my dress. So it took almost no time to bunch the covers to my knees and let my fingers trail lower.

I may not know much about sex, besides what I took away from my awkward first time, but I knew this. I knew me. My wants, my needs. And since I couldn't have the person I wanted the most, then I would have to deal with my own fingers.

I slipped fingertips over my clit, ignoring the sharp pull there as I skimmed lower to tease over my pussy. I didn't know if the adrenaline got my engine going or if it was just being here, so close to Asher, but I was wet.

Wet and begging.

I slipped my fingers there, letting one finger slick lower to tease at the entrance then dragging them high once more. The simple caress made my back bow and my fingers curl away, almost afraid to let myself feel too much.

I needed the distraction, not just the orgasm, and I wasn't ready to let my body fall off the edge of need so quickly.

After a moment, I grew brave enough to let my fingers find my clit again, gently circling the little bundle as my knees fell wide against the soft sheets.

I bit down on my lip, pressing harder against my clit and then letting my fingers tease downwards once more. Slowly I set a rhythm of teasing and movement that made my eyes roll back in my head as I played my own arousal.

I was getting so close, my body shifting against the bed as my fingers grew firmer, bolder against the wet slide of my skin. My free hand moved from my thigh up to breast, pushing up my nightgown as I went. My nipple beaded, and I played with the tip, tugging a little as my body arched into my hands.

"So close," I whispered into the darkness. I closed my eyes hard, savoring my memories of Asher from the past week. The stunning play of his muscles under his skin as he snuck to and from the shower. The strength in his hands as he pulled me to him tonight. And the way his body had curled into mine, every part of him designed to make me scream with pleasure.

And I came. "Asher!"

I tried to muffle my shout with my fist, suddenly aware I could very well wake up Asher with my noises. My muscles tightened and spasmed, making me curl in on myself in pleasure. When my body finally stopped writing on the bed, I opened my eyes a crack to peep around the room once more. The door was still shut, the lights still dark and dim around me.

Apparently not.

Something close to disappointment settled over my belly. I had halfway expected to open my eyes and see the object of my desires standing there. Now I just felt oddly empty, even with the tremors still working their way through my core and thighs.

My hands fell to the bed once more, and I rolled to my side. My body was relaxed now, but my brain was still buzzing with the insanity of the evening. After a few minutes of watching the digital clock by the bedside tick forward, I swung my legs over and stood.

I'd caught a quick glimpse of his kitchen as I had shuffled in here earlier. I would go grab a drink of water. That was what I needed. Tugging my nightshirt as low as it would go, I opened my door and crept out into the apartment, eyes fast on the kitchen.

There was under-cabinet lighting that beckoned me closer, and I was only in the kitchen a few moments before I found both a glass for my drink and a cabinet full of protein shakes, bars, and absolutely no good snacks.

With a huff, I stood on my tiptoes to check another cabinet. Surely the man had something hidden somewhere. As I looked into another barren shelf, there was a low, deep groan from behind me.

An instant later, huge, warm hands fastened themselves around my waist and pulled me fast back to thick, solid man. It was Asher. I could smell him, recognize the feel of him. Not just the physical touch, but the aura he sounded himself with. That intense, all-consuming air of possession.

"Are you trying to kill me, angel?" he growled against my hair.

My body was quaking and not at a single bit with fear. He was shirtless, and the flesh that was pressing against my legs was also bare. My jaw loosened. Was he naked?

I dared to glance down and saw a tiny sliver of dark fabric. He was covered, or at least a little bit. Not that it did anything to hide the rigid length of him that was pressing into the small of my back.

"Ki-Kill you? What do you mean?" The words were garbled in my mouth as one of his hands moved across my belly.

"I finally get to sleep, congratulating myself on resisting you for another day, but then I heard you call out. I knew what you were doing. I knew. And then God help me, I heard you call out my name."

Asher shuddered against me. "My name, from your lips. And I could only imagine why."

"I—" I started, but he turned my face to him with a hand on my jaw, his gaze desperately searching for mine.

"But still, I persisted, not letting myself dream for one instant that it was you, pleasuring yourself to thoughts about me. I thought it was safe enough to walk in here, to take a breath, and here you are, in my shirt." His hand smoothed down the front of my shirt. "And those perfect cheeks peeking out the bottom."

I blushed but remained silent.

His fingers played with the hemline of my borrowed shirt. "Do you deny it, then?"

I could barely put two words together right now. I was distracted by the feel of his knuckles brushing the skin of my thighs, where he toyed with the fabric. I shook my head, feeling my hair brush over my cheeks. "Deny what?"

"That you were touching yourself, thinking about me." Asher stepped closer, eliminated the already small gap between us.

I arched my back, loving the hiss he let out as the delicious friction between us grew. It was now or never. My body screamed for me to move or to make him move. "Why don't you find out for yourself?"

His hot breath blew out over my ear, and one of his fingers stroked up and down my thigh. I groaned, tilting my head back to rest against his chest. Then warm, firm fingers slipped between my legs and pressed against my pussy.

I was still wet there, dripping from my orgasm and from the onslaught of need he'd just whipped up.

"Christ, Lillian." His voice was ragged. "All of this is for me?"

I didn't need to answer. My body already had, grinding down on his hands as he cupped me there.

"Sweet girl, I had no idea you were aching so badly." Asher's hand on my waist tightened, and I felt his cock against my back again. "Let me help."

"Asher?" The question in my voice stilled him for only a moment, and then he pulled away. I meant to protest, to tell him how badly I need him, when I was turned quickly, and his hands scooped me up to drop me on the edge of the countertop.

The cold granite made me flinch, but only for a moment, because then Asher was there. His lips trailing up my inner thighs until he could brush his mouth against where I ached for him most.

I dug my hand hard into his hair, my other hand reaching for the edge of the counter. Anything to center myself against this assault on my senses.

"Asher, I don't know," I started, my stumbling mind trying to put thoughts together, namely the confession that it had been years since I'd been with anyone. And even before then, no man had done what it looked like he was about to do.

His mouth slowed its assault, pulling back ever so slightly. "Are you nervous?"

I nodded.

"Speak up, Lillian. My eyes are busy elsewhere."

I swallowed hard, my hips busy seeking him out even as I held him at a distance. "I'm afraid that…" I gulped, too embarrassed to spit the words out.

Asher turned his head and placed a rumbling chuckle against my pelvis. "Are you worried about how you will taste?"

I nodded again then remembered his earlier command. "Yes," I said, the word small.

His chest rumbled with another chuckle, which made me huff in embarrassment and attempt to slip back farther onto the countertop. His laughter died, his hands tightening on my thighs. With a growl, he dug into the softness of my legs and yanked me back to the edge, back to his mouth.

His tongue slipped out and dipped into the space between my thighs, the heat of it splitting me and making my head fall back in a silent shout.

"Don't you hide from me, angel," he growled before licking me again, starting low and delving deep into me and then continuing up to swirl his tongue around my clit. "And you never have to worry about what you taste like. You taste like honey, and I'm done resisting my sweet tooth."

With that, he sealed his lips over my clit and sucked hard.

Oh my God!

***

Asher

There was no going back now. Not until I felt her cum on my tongue or heard the cries of my name on her lips again.

I wasn't sure how I'd ever resisted in the first place. But tonight, something in me had crumbled the moment I heard her call my name out. The part of my person that was devoted to my job, he knew that once and for all there was no chance to deny what was between us.

Lillian was made for me.

And after this, I would work as hard as possible to be the man she needed. The man she wanted. Even as I bent over her, my mouth working the slick folds between her legs, I knew that it would be worth it.

My life would be loud, chaotic, and more than a little unpredictable, but suddenly my entire being craved that. I'd known that even walking back into my bedroom tonight after sending her to hers. The bed was too cool, the room barren, and the apartment quiet.

There was no humming television, no sheet music lying around the floor, and no Lillian filling the space around her with that quiet joy. And now I craved them, almost as much as I knew I would forever crave the taste of her on my tongue.

I would make her mine. Tonight. It didn't matter that I'd only known her a few weeks. I'd been waiting for her for my entire life.

And I could only hope she felt the same way. Because at the moment, her beautiful body writhing under me was the best thing I'd ever seen in all my thirty-six years.

Yes, I had the right idea. I would vanquish any doubts about her taste with her orgasm on my tongue. And then I would take her to my bed and then lavish every inch of her body with my mouth. By the time I filled her up with my cock, she would be begging for me.

I tongued deep into her pussy, my mind consumed with the fantasy of what she might feel like. Would my clever little flutist be loud in bed? Or would be silently coil around me when she came? I already knew it would be impossible to pull out of her. I wouldn't have the control, especially since every part of me rejoiced in the idea of filling her up.

I wanted her to be full of me for hours. Then I would fill her again, erasing any doubts in her mind.

Her thighs shook on either side of my head, and I knew I was close to seeing nirvana. I curled my hand closer so that I could push a careful finger into her sweet heat while I swirled my tongue around her eager little clit again.

"Asher," she moaned, her fingertips tugging on my dark hair as she ground her body against my face. I groaned, giving in completely as I suckled on that swollen nub, feeling the trembling clench of her inner muscles around my finger.

"Come for me, angel. Let me hear you."

"I can't," she whimpered.

"You can," I challenged and then scraped my teeth over her once. That was all it took to feel the ecstasy spread through her body, making her body quake against mine. Her knees snapped up, hugging my ears as I gently licked her through her orgasm, mentally logging every sound, every taste of her against my mouth.

I wanted to remember it all.

And then I wanted to make her do it ten more times. But not now. I didn't think I could last any longer. My cock wanted in on this action so badly that I could barely straighten my body after pulling away from her.

Her legs dropped as I stood, and she faced me. My borrowed shirt was bunched to her waist, her slender arms were gripping the edge of the countertop, and her face was pink with swollen, flushed lips.

She was perfect.

Chapter 8

Asher

"Gorgeous," I said softly.

Lillian jerked her chin up, and for a moment, I wasn't sure what she was going to do. Run back to her room, pretend this never happened. Or would she come to me now, let me seal this vow in our hearts that we'd been holding out on?

She scooted her ass to the edge of the counter and then looked me up and down, warm brown eyes centering in on the heavy erection that was tenting out my boxer briefs as I stood there. I held still, letting her eyes drink their fill. But inside I could feel the throb of my barely repressed need.

Need to fuck her.

Need to claim her.

Need to fill her up until her belly was swollen and round with my baby.

My knees twitched, and I almost groaned out loud. Where had that thought come from? I couldn't deny that was what my cock wanted, which meant that it was something else I wanted too. At least subconsciously.

I stared back at her, waiting, mentally adding that swollen belly to the delicious picture she made perched in front of me. She was completely edible like this. But with a belly and my seed growing in her belly, she would bring me to my knees with a simple look.

I couldn't wait for the chance, and my words slipped out before I could stop them. "What now, angel?"

Her lips bowed and curled as she met my gaze once more. She lifts her arms to me, spreading her knees wide again. "Take me to bed, Asher. I need you."

I moved in, letting my arms fasten around her as I picked her up off the counter. Her legs snapped closed around me, and I knew instinctively that was where her legs were going to stay for a good chunk of our night. Because now that I could feel the wet heat of her body on my belly, I knew I only had a few brain cells holding me back from plunging into her right now.

But we made it to my bed, and rather than lay her down gently, I crooked a knee and let us tumble into the covers together.

Lillian squealed but hauled me ever closer, gravity acting as my wingman as her body naturally slipped down mine. I could feel the slick from her body resting atop my cock, with only a thin layer of fabric between us.

"Fuck," I growled. "You have two seconds to get this shirt off so I can see those beautiful breasts of yours."

Lillian sprang into action, rising to her elbows to battle the restraining top from her body. When she dropped back flat under me, her breasts, larger than I might have imagined, jiggled.

I panted a little, shifting to her side so I could move to the position I wanted. "Good God, Lillian, these are gorgeous." I fastened my lips around one soft, dusky pink nipple and sucked it lightly into my mouth.

Her body arched into mine, and encouraged, I sucked harder. She was heat and silk under my body, and I pretended to not notice that her free hand and a leg were successfully ridding me of my underwear.

I released her nipple with a soft *pop* and leaned across her to give the same attention to its twin. "Something you need?" I asked between mouthfuls. I couldn't remember the last time I was playful in bed. But this came naturally, this give and take between us.

"Asher, quit messing around," she hissed at me, her fingers insistent and needy against my shoulder now.

I smiled against her skin. "Patience is a virtue."

"Not right now it isn't," Lillian said, her voice tight.

"You're going to need to be nice and soft and wet for me, so trust me and let me get you ready."

She grew still under me. I suckled away on her breasts, letting my fingers trail up and down her ribs as our bodies moved against each other.

"It's been a long time. Will you be gentle?" she said, her breath hot against my jaw.

I gritted my teeth. "I'll be gentle for you."

Her nails suddenly scraped against my side. "And when I want you to be rough?"

"I'm yours to command, Lillian. Always."

Her breathless laugh drew my gaze back down to her face. She looked up at me with such profound longing that I almost came then, just knowing how badly she wanted me.

"Then I need you inside me, Asher. Now." After a second, she added, "Please."

I was powerless to refuse her, and as I parted her thighs to settle between them, I could feel my heart beating erratically in my chest. Reaching between us, I ran the head of my cock between her folds. She was ready.

Sinking in the first few inches was a test in my control, but as my body disappeared into hers, inch by inch, I was overcome with not only the perfection of the feeling of her heat gripping me, but at the rapture and excitement in her eyes.

And when I hesitated, slowing as she became even more tight, I pressed my forehead against hers, breathing her in.

I met her eyes.

"All the way," she commanded me, her legs winding up and around my hips.

I lowered my lids, a hand on her hip and the other on the headboard behind her. I thrust hard, sinking myself deep into Lillian, and finally, at long last, made us one.

***

Lillian

Surprise wasn't the right word. Shock? Maybe. Because as I lay there, every inch of Asher's enormous cock shoved deep into my body, my mind was bombarded with overwhelming emotions.

Pleasure, because sweet Jesus, he felt like heaven. Sure, there was some stretching and more than a little pressure. But as soon as he retreated, dragging that long, heavy cock back over my sensitive muscles, I begged for him to return.

"Oh God," I chanted over and over, my body curling up to seek him out. This part was harder, more awkward as I attempted to catch up with his movements.

Everything he did left me in a literal puddle of feelings and need. But what I offered him? It was way less in the area of experience.

I rolled my hips, desperate to keep more of that ricocheting pleasure. What I lacked in experience, I would make up for in enthusiasm. I crossed my ankles around his body and rolled my hips his direction.

The gasp on his lips made my confidence soar. I did it again, rolling and clenching my thighs as I did. I could feel every inch of him this way. It was addicting, this power I suddenly held over this formidable, opinionated man.

"Lillian," he gritted out, the words tortured and nearly unintelligible.

I held him tighter, my body flush with need as my orgasm came barreling towards me. I wanted to take him with me this time. I wanted to steal his words, his breath, like he had mine.

There was no other option.

Sweet, shy little Lillian was gone. I was a wild thing now, my hips jerking up and down against his cock as he drove himself between my legs. I reared up to clamp my teeth right around his shoulder, holding tight to the tang of his sweaty skin as his hips pounded into me.

"Fill me up, Asher," I whispered against his ear. And I meant it. It was all I could imagine now, the heat of him inside me. I wanted to feel him explode, to mark me as his in the most primal of ways.

My pussy throbbed as I clenched down on him. Oh my God... My own thoughts were about to send me over the edge.

Asher pulled back, a hand tanging in my hair to pry me back so that we met eye to eye as his body worked mine. His gaze was coal back as he stared down at me.

"You look so perfect taking my cock, sweet Lillian. How did I not know how perfect you'd be? Going to have me addicted to the feel of you."

I groaned, my orgasm licking at the back of my mind as I rolled my hips up to him once more. "I need you, Asher. All of it."

"Fuck." Asher's neck and jaw went completely rigid, the muscles there standing out sharp and stark under his olive skin. His hips pumped again, slow now, slapping hard against my clit as he bore down on me. "Take it, angel. Take all of it."

I came in a blinding spasm of pleasure, hard enough that I contorted on the bed under his huge, thrusting body. I was glad for his hold on my hair, as he grounded me, held me under him as my body clenched against him over and over. Distantly I felt when he gripped me, his belly flexing against my body as he grunted, pumping his orgasm into my body with great heaves of his body.

As I slowly floated back to reality, I wondered how he could be so aware, while also losing all control. My hands fluttered up to his shoulders, finding the heavy column of his neck where it was bowed over me.

"Are you alright?"

A soft chuckle. "That's my line."

I smiled into the dark curls of his head. "Even so. Are you?"

His head rose slowly, revealing the handsome face I'd become so enamored with. "I don't think so, Lillian."

Panic gripped my heart as I started to rise up to an elbow. "What... Asher?"

He didn't release me. Instead, he pressed me harder into his mattress. "Hold on. I only meant that you've completely ruined me." Tender, gentle hands brushed the hair away from my face. "It's never been like that for me."

"Really?"

"Really." Asher shifted, and his cock, which had been semisoft inside me still, throbbed gently. "It's been a long time since I've been with someone I cared about."

The look on his face was so sincere that for a moment, I was almost nervous and shy again. How could this man—this beautiful, successful man—want to be with a struggling woodwind player? The idea was preposterous.

Even still, I moved under him, and the shift in the bed made Asher groan deep in his chest. "Be careful, Lillian."

"But we just..."

"It doesn't mean that I want you any less."

I huffed, knowing that my cheeks were pink again. "What now?"

"Now? I hold you here, protect you in your dreams."

"And then?"

"If you wake up, then I'll make you come so hard you'll forget about ever being scared."

I shivered a little at the truth in his gaze.

"I'm good with that."

Asher grinned. "Finally, we agree on something."

***

Lillian

I slept better last night than I had in weeks. Even since before I'd found out about my mystery stalker. And I had a sneaking suspicion that it had everything to do with the pair of muscular arms that were clasped around me right now.

Asher's arms. I shivered just looking down at them, my finger wandering up and down the pronounced veins in his forearms. I'd never thought of forearms as sexy before I met this man. Now I couldn't stop thinking about them. The way the muscles rolled and bunched as he worked over my body last night.

The memory was enough to send a delicious warm tingle straight down to my belly, where it grew and grew until I squirmed my hips against Asher's.

"Angel, you're playing with fire."

I smiled, turning my face into the pillow to muffle the squeak of pleasure at hearing his raspy morning voice against my spine. It had been real. *He* was real.

This, I thought, moving my hips again, was real.

"I've always been a bit of a pyro."

"Clearly," Asher sighed, reclaiming his arm from my grip so he could trace up and down the smooth line of my hip under the sheet. "Did you sleep well?"

I nodded.

Asher pressed a soft kiss against the back of my shoulder. "And not sore?"

That heat in my belly only grew. "I'm not sure." I hid the smile on my face, imaging what was about to come next.

Firm, strong hands turned me over onto my back. I chirped in false surprise as Asher's worried gaze swept over my body once, twice, not even lingering on my now bared breasts.

"Did I hurt you? Where did I hurt you?" On hand moved over me now, fingertips sweeping across my skin as if searching for the source of my pain. My composure broke, and I giggled.

"Asher, I'm sorry. I was just going to tease you."

Asher's eyes turned dark. "You are never allowed to tease me about your health. Alright? Everything else is free game."

He leaned in to press his mouth against my navel. "But never you."

The shaking emotion in his voice made me bite my lip.

I slid one hand into his mussed curls, tugging until he gave up his kissing of my belly to meet my eyes. "I'm sorry, Asher. I understand."

He nodded. Then in a split second, the entire atmosphere in the room flipped and a broad smile curled his lips.

"You snore."

My jaw dropped. "I do not."

His eyebrow quirked. "Oh yes. Yes, you do."

"Well, you..." I looked him over, muscle after muscle stacked on his torso, the sheet scrunched up against his hips, beautiful jawline covered with a dark scruff. He was fucking perfect. Dammit. "You steal the blankets."

His smile only grew. "Is that so? We'll see about that." Rocking back onto his heels, he gave the sheets between us a quick yank and exposed us both to the morning air.

"Asher!" I squealed, my hands instinctively grabbing for the rest of the sheets. I'd been bold last night, with the dim lighting and his body covering mine. That was very different than the bright Chicago sunlight that blazed in from the window over our shoulders.

Now he could see everything.

The sheets were gone, so I settled for covering my face with my hands, pretending that I wasn't horrified at this stunning specimen see me like this.

A long breath passed, and my horror was slowly replaced by curiosity. The man hadn't moved an inch. I peeked between my fingers, interest finally winning out.

Asher had sat back on his heels, his gaze all over my body. But instead of a lecherous smile, or even his trademark smirk, there was something else on his face. He must've seen my hands move, because he leaned over me, pressing his mouth against one hipbone then the other. Then he rose up to press his mouth to my belly and then higher to the valley between my breasts. The kisses were soft, reverent.

By the time he sat back again, my thighs were shaking with the effort to not drop my knees wide and beg him to settle there. Or even better, to kiss me there again.

"Lillian, you are gorgeous."

I squirmed, feeling the heat in my skin as I flushed. I opened my mouth to rebuke him, but I stopped. Or rather, he stopped me with the look he sent me.

"I wasn't finished." He gave me a quick smile, but his face was serious. Crawling up to situate himself at my side, he ran his fingers over my body again. "I see a beautiful face, breasts that make me want to fall to my knees, hips made to carry babies and tease my control, and legs that are exactly the right length to wrap around my waist."

His eyes flickered to mine then dropped to my lips. "I could show you, if you don't believe me."

"I believe you."

Asher nodded, settling back on the bed. "Good."

"But..." I blushed as I pushed up over him. "You could still show me if you wanted."

One side of his smile pulled up. "If I wanted? Angel, I would sell my soul for a chance to taste you again."

I bit my lip, feeling bold. "You don't need to sell your soul." I shifted and slung my leg over his body so that I was sitting, naked as the day I was born, on top of the ridges of his belly.

Who was I?

I pressed my fingers into his chest and leaned to his ear. "But I would accept a shower."

Asher's eyes went black. "Your wish is my command."

With a soft grunt, we were vertical, me clinging to him as he marched both of us into his adjoining bath. The door closed, and instead of letting me down, his hands found the curve of my ass and cupped me ever closer.

"Is that all you needed?"

I bit my lip, looking down into his handsome face. "I mean, not quite."

Chapter 9

Asher

If I wasn't hard as fucking stone, I might have laughed. When I'd asked her what else she needed, I'd expected her to tease and flirt back to me, and then I was going to trap her against my bathroom door and run my cock through those slick, hot folds between her legs until both of us were dying to complete the action.

However…that was not my Lillian.

So now we were staring at each other, still naked, me still hard, as we brushed our teeth. I ran the bristles over my molars one last time before leaning over and spitting out the toothpaste. Rinsing my mouth, I turned to watch her complete the same action.

A strange, heavy weight pressed against my shoulders once more. Domestic. We'd been living together for just over a week, and it was already ten times more serious than any other relationship I'd ever managed. Even the ones I had dragged on for a long period of time. Because Lillian was endgame.

Which meant things would be changing. And as I watched Lillian carefully put her toothbrush in the cup next to mine, I suddenly couldn't wait.

Change was good.

This change was good.

Because I would be hers.

I'd belonged to people constantly. I spent my life in their offices, their houses, even their vacations. I'd never had my own before.

Lillian was mine. She was fighting over toothpaste flavors. And cute little snores in the night. And as insane as it might sound, I think she wanted me back.

Her amber eyes met mine in the mirror, and she turned to me almost shyly. I hid my grin, knowing it would only embarrass her more.

"Done?"

Lillian shrugged. "Yeah, I'm good."

"Good." I closed the distance between us and leaned in to wrap my arms around her, picking her back up to where we started.

She giggled against my shoulder, sharp little nails digging into my shoulder as I walked us to the shower. I turned the knob, and water started down from the rainwater head.

"Asher, what are you doing?"

"You, my little angel, are very, very dirty."

I only had a moment to savor the shocked look on her face before I stepped under the still-cool water.

Her legs tightened as she pressed against my chest, attempting to hide from the water as it came to temperature.

"Asher," she whispered, sputtering in the water.

"Hush. Let me." The water was warm now, and I slowly released her so that she stood in front of me, her pebbled nipples pressing against my skin as I gripped a bar of soap and slowly ran it over her body.

She practically purred as I soaped her down, letting the hot water wash the suds off her beautiful body. Mentally I took note of every place and part of her that seemed especially sensitive. I would be spending more time with those areas soon.

I slipped a leg between hers and almost came when she scooped up some of the suds and ran them over the head of my cock.

"Easy, baby. I can't handle your hands on me right now."

Lillian pouted up at me. "What?"

I trapped her hand in mine, dragging it down my stomach until we wrapped around the head of my cock together. "You feel like heaven to me. But I'm too selfish for that right now. I'm not coming anywhere but inside this sweet little body. There's plenty of time for that later."

I released her hand and washed off the rest of the soap. Pulling her with me, I dropped my hips until I sat on the small shower bench on one side of the large walk-in. The plastic was cold, but I was desperate to feel her around me again.

"Come here," I told her, tugging her after me.

Eyes bright, Lillian moved to stand on either side of my knees, her belly quivering as I held her there, making the air grow hot and tense between us.

"What are you looking at?" Lillian asked, her voice a little exasperated.

I smirked up at her. "What is mine."

That stole the irritation straight from her lips. Her knees bent, wanting to take me into her body now. And for a breath, I almost allowed it. My cock demanded it, throbbing from between our bodies.

I reached out slowly, slipping my fingers between her legs, to caress the satiny folds of her sex. "Because this is mine now." I looked up at her, watching her chest heave. I moved my hand up, pressing across her belly. "And this." I continued going upward until I traced the outline of one perfect breast and then the other. "And these."

I shifted, reaching up and gripping the underside of her jaw. The delicate line of her neck fit right into my palm. I squeezed ever so slight, making her look down at me. "You are mine."

A shiver racked her delicate form. "Yours," she responded softly, her vocal cords vibrating gently against my hand.

I released my hold to grip her hips and guide her down. Inch by inch, I sank into the sweetness of her core. The heat of her pussy made everything else in the world grow blurry and gray as I became absorbed into her.

She slowed as her legs bent, her mouth wide with surprise as she rode me for the first time. I hitched her closer, and when she slowed, still a small distance from the base, I growled, found the soft flesh her thighs, and guided her down as I ground my hips up.

"Ahh!" Lillian cried out softly, her head falling back as she took every inch of me. Our skin pressed together in a slick mess of need.

"That's my girl," I crooned to her, my hands tightening once again on her thighs.

"Yes, oh God, Asher." Her slender fingers grappled across my shoulders before they found my wet, hanging curls.

An idea rooted in my mind, dark and heavy. "Tell me, my angel, what kind of birth control are you on?"

Silence surrounded my question, only broken by the continuing rush of the water from the shower as she panted against me. Brown eyes, anxious and wild, met mine. My heart soared, knowing the answer before she ever spoke the words.

"My pills… They're back at my apartment."

I groaned, fire licking at my brain as I rolled my cock up into the heat of her body. Whatever her thoughts were, she wasn't willing to stop, as Lillian immediately rolled her body to meet mine once more.

"Good," I growled, yanking her torso closer so I could paint the side of her neck with my tongue, tasting the salt that still lingered there. "Did you want me to pull out? Is that what you're thinking about now?"

Lillian bounced heavily on her feet, pressing her breasts towards my mouth as she did. The picture of luxurious need. I savored every tug of my hair as she rode me harder, her face tightening as she considered my words.

Because there was no way she hadn't heard them.

Pleasure, different than what burned up through my groin, blossomed in my chest. The thought of filling her full, of making sure every part of her was covered in my cum, made my head spin. I'd never felt like this before, and at the same time I wasn't surprised. Because it seemed like the only natural reaction.

I wanted to cover her in my essence, to watch her drip with my cum, and take her again and again until she was perfectly swollen with my baby. Then I would worship her.

My cock twitched as I imagined curling in my bed, her big belly pressing against me as we slept. Maybe I would feel the kicks of life under her satin skin, the next part of our lives calling out to me.

It was all there, laid out before me, begging me to take it.

I reached forward, my hands full of her breasts as I thrust up into her sweet cunt. "Because I think you love it. I think you're begging for my cum, my seed. That you want to feel it fill you up once again, knowing that every secret part of you is covered in me. Because you're mine."

Lillian's head bobbed back, her hips jerking once more against my cock as the tight muscles began to clench around me. "Asher..." Lillian's soft voice was ragged.

"Come for me, beautiful. Take it all."

I could feel the moment her orgasm overtook her, the sharp pinprick of her nails on my shoulders. Then there was the utterly delightful look on her face as she stared right into my eyes, her mouth falling open as she quivered and shook around me.

"Sweet angel," I said, grunting softly as I followed her, pleasure nearly blinding me as I thrust up into that soft, willing body over and over again.

When we finally stilled, there was nothing but the two of us, our hearts racing, our fingers still tightly clenched against each other.

I knew then that Lillian Oakes was the only woman in the entire world for me.

***

Lillian

Did I look thoroughly fucked?

Because that's how I felt. I felt like every time I looked in a mirror, or really any reflective surface, the woman looking back was flushed with pleasure, like she had just orgasmed her way through an entire week.

Which, honestly, was the truth.

Because once Asher and I broke through that pesky professional boundary, there was no going back. There was the shower, the bed, the floor, the window by the fire escape, even the private rooftop deck.

I had seen them all. I had come on them all. Each and every one leaving a tiny dent in the shell that I had tried to put between myself and Asher Brooks. And after a week of living in Asher's penthouse with him, that shield was about two seconds from crumbling all together.

But I had to hold it together tonight. Our final performance of the season and the last in my contract. I wasn't sure how it happened, but this was what it all came down to. My performance tonight could make or break my future at the symphony. If I didn't come back for another year, I wasn't sure what I would do.

And there was a strange sort of yearning that accompanied that. My entire life had been planned for this. Since I was in fourth grade and picked up the flute, I had been primed for this exact instance.

I took a huge breath in, letting it out just like Asher had showed me. "Baby steps, Lillian," I coached myself.

Then I flushed again because my ridiculously handsome bodyguard never failed to remind me how badly he wanted to get me pregnant. Even after that first time in the shower, I'd assumed he'd consider it just sex talk and nothing would come of it.

Except when my things had arrived from my apartment, he continued to hide my pills around the apartment, attempting to distract me as I went hunting for them. And when we curled up together at night, I caught him pressing a hand over my abdomen, feeling the softness of my belly as the haze of the night slipped over me.

I wasn't against having babies. I loved kids and always pictured myself having enough for an entire family band, but I'd only known Asher a few weeks. My eyes slid shut, picturing my bodyguard.

It seemed fast.

But also…oh, so right.

Regardless, I knew, thanks to my careful googling, that it wasn't very likely for him to get me pregnant this month. So, in the meantime, I was going to let my freak flag fly. The idea of him getting me pregnant, breeding me as he towered over my prone body, was nothing that I'd ever considered.

And I had a strong feeling I would crave it forever. Even now, my thighs clenched at the thought of that tall, muscular body, quaking in between my thighs, his eyes wild as he came deep inside me.

I took a long, shuddering breath.

"Shit."

"A dirty mouth on my angel," someone said, and I opened my eyes to Asher standing behind me. He was dressed in an untouchable black suit, his jawline sharp and golden in the soft light of his bedroom. My thighs clenched again, and the giant smirked at me.

It was like he knew what I was thinking.

"I do know what you're thinking," he answered calmly.

I gasped, turning to swat at his shoulders. "Stop that mind-reading stuff."

"Stop making it so easy," Asher said, catching my hands easily and yanking me closer to his body so he could seal his mouth over mine in a long, soft kiss.

I was going to definitely need that birth control next month, or else there would be a baby Brooks on the way before the month was out. No joke about that.

I pulled away, pressing a hand against his chest. We'd agreed on only one thing, that this, whatever this was, it was serious. First, we had to get rid of this stupid stalker, and then we would give this relationship a real test drive.

And if Asher had his way, he'd have me introduced to his family and pregnant before the summer was out.

It was weird to say that I had no problem with that. In fact, if he hadn't come up with that plan, I just might have.

Asher raked his gaze up and down my body. "You look stunning."

I ignored the flush of heat that was my blush. "We have to go."

"Spoilsport," Asher teased, but his hands dropped from me to straighten his tie. "At least I get to escort in such a beautiful performer."

I rolled my eyes, taking his hand and using it to step into my heels. "You get to walk in the leper with a stalker, but let's not talk about that."

I meant it to be teasing, but the comment was like ice over a fire, Asher's face immediately going still, his hand in my grip going stiff and cool.

My heart leaped to my throat.

"Nothing will happen to you. I promise you, Lillian."

I turned to him, pressing a hand against the hard plane of his chest. "I know. You'll be there to protect me."

I meant for him to smirk or even give me a small smile. Instead, it was only a small, short nod. I gulped in response. I'd almost forgotten what professional Asher was like.

And how much danger I was really in.

But it didn't matter tonight. Tonight, I performed for my career.

Chapter 10

Lillian

I milled around the side of the stage, Asher at my shoulder as I looked out into the crowd. It was packed, and since I hadn't been out in crowds for week, it suddenly seemed to be too much. I wanted my tiny little apartment with Asher on the couch. I would even take Asher's luxurious king-sized bed with its mountain of pillows.

Anything but this.

I gulped. When had I lost the love for performance? I'd enjoyed every practice session, every discussion on the musical choices. But tonight, this was suddenly my nightmare. What had changed?

I wasn't sure.

A heavy hand dropped onto my shoulder, reminding me that I wasn't stewing alone but rather standing three feet from my very large, very overprotective bodyguard. I looked up at him, cocking my head.

Boyfriend? The word didn't seem right. It didn't seem significant enough for some reason. Asher wasn't "boyfriend" material. He hadn't been lying about that in the least. He was…well…intense. Maybe lover?

I gave an involuntarily shudder. That word was just cringy for some reason. Sounded like something out of my mother's historical romances.

He was just Asher. And he was mine.

I smiled at that. I liked that the best out of everything so far. *Mine.*

"Are you ready?"

"Almost." I looked around, disappointed that Tiffany was still not back. The police had uncovered more details about her stalker but still hadn't managed to track down the man responsible. I dearly missed my friend. I wished I could tell her about this sudden resurgence of anxiety and worry over performing. She would always have the exact right thing to say.

I leaned against Asher for just an instant, and I could feel the hesitation in his body as we touched. Here, tonight, I was still just his client and him my bodyguard.

"Oh my gosh." I spun in a small circle, looking around the floor for my missing necklace. "Asher, my necklace."

"You had it on when we left the apartment."

I clearly remembered that. He'd slipped the necklace on me himself, taking the moment to kiss and touch every part of my bare skin that was exposed by my dress. There wasn't much, but he'd savored every bit of it. Enough that I'd almost shoved him back in bed and shown him just how grateful I was for all the recent support and affection.

"Maybe it got caught up when I redid my hair. I have to go back!" I shot across the small space, searching for the narrow hall that would take me back to the dressing area.

"No way, Lillian. We've already moved everyone out into the audience. I don't have coverage for you back there."

My stupid lip trembled. "Asher, I need it. It's my good-luck charm. I've never not worn it at a concert."

"You don't need it. You're an amazing performer. No necklace will change that."

I sniffled, pressing my hand against my lips to stifle the tears. I was not going to ruin my makeup just for this.

"Asher, please."

I knew my eyes were filling with tears, but somehow tonight, this seemed like something I couldn't get by without. I'd worn it for every performance since fifth grade.

I could see the debate in his eyes, and he quickly swept the area, taking note of everything—every other performer, every backstage employee. Then, with a rattling growl, his hand found the back of my head, dragging me forward to his body. I propped my hands on his suit, surprised and pleased by the signs of possession.

"Stay here. Do not go anywhere or do anything until I get back," he growled. "Do you hear me?"

I nodded, pressing my hands to his chest in silent gratitude.

With a grimace, Asher turned, his watch immediately at his lips as he spoke into the technology. He was probably triggering Joey, who was the only AXE security team member I had met before. He was acting as a guest out in one of the front rows.

I took a long, rattling breath. Asher would return in a moment with my necklace. I would step onto this stage like I owned it, even if I had forced the feeling. I owed that much to Tiffany.

"Curtain in ten. Everybody to their seats," someone bellowed behind me.

I flinched. I would much rather risk the symphony's ire than Asher's, so I was planning on waiting it out here until he returned. The backstage hallway was winding but I guessed he would be back in a matter of a few minutes.

Some friends moved by, smiling at me as I resisted the instinct to follow suit. More than a few changed their expression as they settled into their spaces, eyeing my position on the sidelines.

I could feel my face flushing as I stood there, twiddling my thumbs idly. I wanted my flute in my hand. I wanted that comfort. I eyed my seat, wondering what Asher would do to me if I deliberately disobeyed him over this.

Just as I picked up my foot to step onto the stage, a blaring alarm came over the intercom. "There has been a fire detected on the premises. Please follow exit signs to safety."

My heart hammered.

Because not only did the idea of the fire send fear shooting down my spine, but more than that, something seemed too close for comfort. On the night I finally returned, there was an emergency.

It wasn't likely? Right?

I watched as the director and a few emboldened percussionists ushered the performers off the other side of the stage. Cold, icy fear made my heart hammer in my chest.

"Asher?" I called over my shoulder. He should be here any moment. The last of the other performers were leaving the stage, and I couldn't see Joey anymore.

At this point, I was more than happy to risk being in trouble with my growling roommate than to stay on this empty stage alone. I turned, my heels making little clicking noises as I exited the stage and fumbled backstage. The hallway was empty. Obviously all the stagehands were already exiting.

"Asher!" I yelled once more, louder and harsher than before. Incredibly, at the very end of the hall, the space of roughly of one hundred twenty feet or so, Asher appeared. His tie was crooked and there was something just haggard about him, but he was standing.

Adrenaline and very real fear compelled me forward. And just like the night I first met him, I focused my entire being on getting to Asher.

He was safety. He was strength. I needed to be with him. Fear clogged my throat as I ran, even as Asher too began to sprint towards me. His gaze was intense on me, his face frozen in an effort to cover as much space as possible.

That's probably why he didn't see the man step out from one of the side rooms, a long, slender bar in his hand.

And there was nothing I could, no noise I could make before he brought it down on Asher's head. My bodyguard hit the ground before the sound could even leave my lips. I slid to a stop, falling to my knees as my stalker moved ever closer.

The masculine form stepped right up to me, running a gentle hand over my head as my chest heaved. Aside from the frantic beating of my heart, my mind was consumed with only one thing.

I had to get out of this myself.

Asher had taught me well. I knew what would likely come next, but I needed to buy time. More time meant more options. I blinked rapidly, staring up into the ski mask–covered face.

"You arranged all of this?"

His head cocked. "Yes. Of course."

"Who are you? What do you want?" My voice was steadier than my heart.

He reached down to grip my arms and guide me to my feet. "You can call me"—he seemed to consider it—"Bach."

For a moment I forgot my fear. "Like the composer?"

The grip on my arms grew tighter. "Yes, like the composer." He shook me a little, beginning to walk towards Asher then ducking into a small hallway I'd never been in.

I craned my head, staring at Asher's unconscious body and hoping that he would be okay. That we would both be okay. Joey should be here any minute. He would help Asher, and they would get me. I just needed to hold on a bit longer.

"And what do you want?" I gritted out, trying to keep up with his rather large, awkward steps. But then, he still had ahold of my shoulder and didn't seem that interested in letting me walk like a normal person. "What did I ever do to you?"

Bach looked at me sharply. I couldn't see the expression, but there was something of surprise in his movement. "You haven't figured it out yet?"

I tripped over some equipment as the room got darker. Bach cursed at me, fingers biting into my flesh as he hauled me up. High-pitched laughter tumbled from his mouth as he stopped us. He was unlocking something. I could hear the sound of a keychain.

Then bright lights blinded me temporarily, stopping only when he stepped back in front of me. "I'm not interested in you. Other than a means to an end."

My heart plummeted through my chest. *Asher, please wake up*, I chanted internally.

"You're going to get her back for me. And you're going to do it tonight."

"Who?"

Bach snarled, his voice gruff with fury. "Tiffany. She's the love of my life, and you ruined it. Now it's time for you to get her back for me."

***

Asher

Someone was screaming my name. I moved my arms, mentally checking for injuries there and only noticing the immense pain at the back of my skull. Everything else responded with a slow, groggy movement as I tested it.

Screaming. Why were they still screaming? Suddenly, heavy, urgent hands grabbed the back of my suit, hauling me over onto my back.

"Fuck!" I shouted, a hand automatically driving backwards to cover the back of my head as they lowered me again.

"Asher," a familiar voice sounded above me. I squinted up at the ugly fluorescent lights, trying to get my eyes to focus on the faces leaning over me.

"Emerson? Why are you here?"

It hit me like a ton of bricks. The fire alarms going off. Getting trapped behind a fire door down by the dressing rooms. And when I'd finally gotten through, I'd seen her and known. Known it wasn't a causal coincidence. That it was exactly what we had feared.

And before I could get to her, that splitting pain at the back of my head.

"You've only been down a few minutes. I was close, but Xavier is on his way too."

"Xavier? Why?" My thoughts were still muddled.

Emerson looked at Joey, whose steady, calm demeanor was starting to wear on my patience. My eldest brother reached out, helping me to sit up, and scoot back against the wall. He went to his haunches in front of me, nodding to Joey, who disappeared down the hall.

Emerson.

Joey.

Xavier.

Fear lit me up like lightning, making every one of my nerves snap to attention. I reached out, gripping Emerson's forearms. "Em, where is Lillian?"

My stoic, solemn brother was quiet, his free hand wiping down his face as if to wipe away any real expression.

"Em?"

"He took her, Asher. We confirmed it on the security cameras."

I stared at him, my body vibrating with barely repressed energy that didn't know where to go. Suddenly my head didn't ache so much.

"Asher, talk to me. What did you see?"

"It doesn't matter," I said, pushing away from my brother. He rose slowly, offering a hand down.

"I expect it won't do any good to tell you to stay down until medics get here?"

I glared at him, slapping my hand into his to let him heave me to my feet. To my body's credit, there was only a split second of shooting pain before the world cleared and I was able to focus again.

Because there was only one thing that mattered now. I looked at my big brother.

"I love her."

He nodded. "I know. Let's go get your girl back."

***

Lillian

Bach didn't go very far with me. I wasn't sure if it was because he could barely wait to get me alone to enact the next step in his plan, or if that was just part of his plan. But after only a few short turns in a plain black SUV, I found myself sitting at a small downtown park. The heavy fencing was closed for the night, but he seemed unconcerned.

He pulled out his phone, poking around on the screen for several minutes before turning to me.

"Here's what you have to do. You're going to call Tiffany. You'll tell her that she needs to come home to Chicago immediately. And that you've met someone really great you want to introduce her to."

"But that will take hours. She can't just get up and walk here. By the time she arrives, it will be tomorrow or later."

"It doesn't matter. Once she's here, she'll understand she belongs with me."

"Does she even know you?" I questioned before I realized how sarcastic my voice had gotten. I bit my lip hard, shifting on my seat as far away from Bach as possible.

"She does. She will understand."

I shivered. "I just have to call her, and then you'll let me go."

The chuckle in his chest made my stomach roll. "We'll see."

I knew immediately what that meant. As long as I was useful, I got to stay here and reasonably safe. As soon as this part of the plan was done, I wasn't useful anymore.

An idea rooted around in my mind. This guy had no idea how much time Tiffany and I had spent staring at each other across a rehearsal space. I could read her like a book. I knew she could do the same.

"Do you want me to call her via Screentime?"

His head jerked up from his phone again.

"She loves Screentime. She always answers that."

Bach tilted his head, looking like a demented fly in the near darkness. My stomach clenched hard, nausea warring at the back of my mind, until finally, he nodded.

"What do I say to get her here?"

Bach palmed the loaded gun that was tucked into his waistband. "Get creative."

I swallowed, nodding. "Now?"

"Now," he growled back, shoving my phone into my hands. "No funny business. You get that one call, so make sure she confirms. Make sure."

I nodded again, my throat sticky and tight with fear. Tiffany was on my most recent calls, and I pressed the button, flinching when Bach slammed his hand against the roof of our unmarked SUV. The tiny interior lightbulb flickered to life.

My gaze jumped to his face, but even now, I couldn't see any features. And when I lingered in my attempt, he leaned over me, growling once more. "Do it!"

I hit the camera button, positioning the phone in front of my face as I smiled into the device. My mind was whirling, trying to figure out how to get my message across to Tiffany.

Of course, she answered immediately, her bouncing brown curls taking up half the screen as she shrieked into the phone. "Lillian, I'm so glad you called! I've been dying to figure out what happened at the show. The live feed is just an empty stage."

I opened my mouth, trying to speak. Nothing came out. I cleared my throat as I felt the not-so-subtle press of a gun barrel against my side once more.

"Fire drill. They had to clear everyone out." I rolled my eyes dramatically. "Crazy, right?"

"Completely." Tiffany pulled back from the screen a little, and I could tell she was at home, curled up on a sofa. My heartbeats double. I may not have been able to get help, but Tiffany could.

"You have got to tell me all about your sexy security situation," Tiffany crooned. "That picture you sent me…it was not enough!"

I smiled, my stomach still churning at the thought of Asher right now. I needed him to be okay. Not just so that he could rescue me, but so that I could spend the next fifty years of my life apologizing for making him retrieve my necklace. "Don't worry. I'll get you some more." My voice came out strained, and I dropped my chin to clear my throat.

"I was actually hoping that you would come home soon. I need your help seducing him."

Tiffany stilled. She knew very well that I'd already slept with Asher. "What?"

"I cannot get the man into bed. He's resistant. Maybe you can come home this weekend and give me some advice? Especially since you're more experienced than me."

I gritted my teeth, wondering if I had gone too far. Tiffany was a virgin, but I was trying to tip her off that something was wrong. It must've worked, since the phone screen was sudden pulled close again and Tiffany was looking at me with sharp, keen eyes.

"Have you been crying?"

I cleared my throat, trying to think of the correct response. "Well, I just told you I needed you help with Asher."

"Yeah...and that I need to come home."

"Yes, immediately."

Tiffany was moving, the screen shifting only slightly.

"You know I love you, right?"

I could see that she was in a living room, and I prayed silently there was someone there who could call for help.

"I love you too, sis." Tiffany's voice was strained now. I tensed; it was getting too obvious. "Tell me, right now, where are you?"

"The park by our favorite ice cream place." I jerked my arm back, elbowing Bach hard in the neck, and then launched myself at the door. I held the phone up to my face as I bailed from the vehicle. "Hurry!"

And then I was running, across the darkened playground, my bare feet digging into the slippery grass. I knew he was coming for me, and my phone slipped from my hand. Tiffany and her screaming voice muffled when they hit the ground.

But I didn't stop running. I had to buy Asher and the AXE team enough time to find me. Just a little longer.

I made it across the equipment before tumbling to my knees. Bach was on me in a minute. We rolled, knees and elbows flying, just like Asher had taught me.

At the last moment, just before his fist hit my face with a resounding thud, I heard another noise. Another voice.

I could've sworn it was Asher's. But before I could call for him, the world went black.

Chapter 11

Asher

"You should let me kill him."

Emerson eyed me, dark eyes unreadable. "Xavier already did quite the number on him."

"Lucky asshole."

"Well-placed asshole." Xavier had been coming to get us from the performance hall when I'd gotten Lillian's tracker working again. He'd beaten Emerson and me here, and while the blood still pumped furiously through me at the thought that it hadn't gotten to be me to peel the man off Lillian, I was grateful to my sibling.

I glanced up at Emerson. Grateful to both of them.

"Thanks for everything tonight."

"You're my brother. You don't have to say anything."

I glanced down at the woman curled in my lap. "Yes, I do."

Lillian had been cleared after Xavier had tackled Bach off her. The cops Tiffany had called from safety in Kentucky had arrived en masse and brought the medics straight there. I smoothed a hand across her tousled hair, wondering how I was going to bring myself to let her go again.

Emerson's hand dropped on my shoulder with a gentle squeeze, saying more with that simple gesture than a thousand words. I clenched my eyes shut.

"Can we go home now?" I asked the paramedic, who was looking at the back of my head. I was going to have one hell of a headache, but nothing was gushing blood and I wanted to get home. I wanted to take Lillian home. To our bed. To our life.

It would be a long time before I would be letting her out of my sight.

"Home?" a soft voice asked. Lillian had awoken, brown eyes dark and worried. She'd already been through enough questioning tonight.

"Yes, home." The paramedic gave me a thumbs-up, so I shifted her, cradling her across my chest as I stood and moved towards the car Xavier had brought. He'd already given me the keys, telling me to get out of here as soon as possible.

There would be more statements for the police. There would be prodding and questioning. But all of that would start after tonight.

Brian Harrell—or Bach, as he called himself--was safely in custody.

The rest could wait.

I gently leaned in to place Lillian in the car.

It was over. Something in my chest twisted as I tucked her in. It was all over.

***

Lillian

I wasn't sure if I'd moved more than ten or so feet since Asher carried me into his bedroom. We showered that first night, and I'd fallen asleep with my now ex-bodyguard wrapped around me.

I'd savored it.

And for the next few days, it'd been pretty much the same ritual. We showered together, his hands slicking up and down my body, taking so much time that the water almost ran cold before we stepped out and fell back into bed.

There was a finality to all of this that I knew both of us were avoiding. Something about leaving this room, this blissful safe space where it was just Asher and me and soft pillows.

When we left, we had to determine how this thing between us was going to work.

When we left, I had to address the very real concern that I had no interest in returning to performance life.

And when we left, we had to address the fact that I'd fallen madly in love with the man I'd paid to guard me.

I'd never planned for any of this. But now I couldn't imagine anything else.

"What are you thinking?"

Asher's lips brushed across my shoulder, the sweet mint of his breath making me smile as I snuggled in closer.

"About what I'm going to do with my life."

Asher's dark brow quirked, and that smirk, which I'd missed so much these past few days, suddenly made a reappearance. I smiled back at him.

"That's quite deep for seven in the morning. I thought we agreed to keep our thoughts to the important areas of life. Eating, sleeping, and finding exactly which spots on your body make you moan the loudest." Playful teeth found my earlobe, and he tugged it.

"Asher," I admonished, trying to sound upset. It didn't work, so I brushed a hand down his forearm.

"Perhaps I should distract you."

"As delightful as it's been, we need to start thinking about what's next."

Asher's kisses continued down my neck, the hot press of his lips making it very hard to focus on the matter at hand.

"Asher Ray Brooks, you need to focus."

"I'm quite focused."

"I mean on things…not me," I said, but my words were breathless, and I rolled onto my back, pressing him aside so that I could stare up into his handsome face.

Asher sighed, settling on an elbow and looking down into my face. "You can't blame me for trying."

"Not at all. Just suggesting we take a quick break to revisit reality and see how it's doing."

"Fine." Asher plucked his phone off the nightstand and scrolled through it for a moment. Then he rolled back towards me, reassuming his earlier position. "My reality sucks. What are you thinking about?"

I giggled, letting my fingers wander up to trace the line of his jaw. It was relaxed now, the stubble there brushing against my skin and making my mind light up with memories of how it had felt against my thighs last night. I blushed red hot.

"I don't want to perform anymore. At least like I was."

"Because of Bach?"

"No, because… I'm not sure. It just doesn't feel right now. Maybe it will again in the future, but for now, I think I'm going to take a step back, take on some students, and enjoy the process a bit more."

"Really?" Asher's eyes were bright on me. "That sounds perfect, angel."

I smiled at him. "I think so too." I could feel the next question get caught in my throat. Because it seemed even bigger than what the defining situation was between Asher and me. Even after all of this, or perhaps especially because of it, I wasn't sure that I was going to be in a situation where I could be with Asher if it meant his life was what our lives had been with Bach. I wanted a real life, a quiet life away from the fear.

I had meant it when I said it to him back in my apartment, and I meant it now.

I swallowed hard, watching as his face changed slowly. He had to know what was on my mind. He had to.

"Asher…what does that mean for you? Does it change anything?"

Asher looked pale, his face tense as he stared down at me. "Lillian, I…I have been wanting to talk to you about something." He paused, waiting until I nodded in encouragement. "I got a job offer this morning, my next case."

I stilled, my body humming with the onslaught of anxiety. We hadn't even been able to discuss it. How did that even work? Frustration gathered behind my eyes, making them water as I blinked up at him.

"How could they? We just barely got through the last week."

"It was from Emerson."

"What? Like, for your brother? How could he?" I was on the edge of throwing myself off the bed to pace around when Asher pressed a hand down over my belly, pinning me in place.

"A favor, yes, but I turned him down."

All thoughts of pacing vanished. "You did?" My heart throbbed heavily in my chest.

Asher nodded. "I did. I turned them all down in fact."

"What does that mean?"

"I took the other job offer Emerson sent. The one from a few months ago."

"To run his recruitment and operations?"

After a long moment, Asher nodded.

"But…" My voice broke so I tried again. "But you didn't want that job."

He leaned in and pressed a soft kiss to my throat. "That wasn't why I turned it down before. As it turns out, I was just waiting until I had found something worth leaving the field for." Asher looked at me hard. "And I found her."

I stared up at him, those pesky tears still fresh in my eyes. "I don't want you to change for me."

"Everyone changes a little, even me, and I'll be honest… The idea of coming home every day to my very own personal concert thrills me."

I giggled a little, happiness making my chest ache.

Asher's face was serious. "I didn't think I'd ever find someone like you, Lillian. Someone who made everything else and everyone else dull in comparison. And I would give it all up to make sure that I could spend even an extra moment a day with you."

For a long, tense moment, we looked up into each other's faces. Then he smirked widely at me. "Plus, this gives me more time to plan the proposal of the century and work on convincing you to have at least four babies."

"Asher!" I squealed as he ducked his head to press a kiss between my breasts. "Four?"

He ignored the tugs I gave his hair and burrowed deeper. "At least four."

"We'll see." I stroked my fingers through his curls, a deep satisfaction rolling through me. "You know, I don't need the big proposal. It's not really my style."

"What?"

"I need the big wedding though. Big family, only daughter… It'll have to happen." I pressed my hand against the side of his face.

Asher nodded seriously, eyes sparkling. "I firmly intend on shaming my brothers into paying for everything."

"Perfect," I said, laughing.

"Do you mean that though? Because I'm committed to making you the happiest woman in the world. You can have the big proposal *and* the big wedding."

"I mean it. I just want to be with you."

Asher stared at me, long and hard. Then bounced to his knees and straddled one of my legs. "Lillian Oakes, you are the center of my world and the reason my heart beats. Marry me and make me the happiest man out there?"

I blinked up at him. "Are you proposing to me now?"

The devil himself smirked down at me. "You said you didn't need the proposal to be a big deal…"

"I mean, yeah, but…Asher, we are both naked."

He grinned at me, morning light making his skin glow. "All the better to ravish my fiancée."

"I didn't say yes yet."

Asher leaned in, pressing kisses up one side of my leg and then over my belly, where held his mouth for an extra moment.

"You will," he said, confident as ever.

"Asshole."

"Angel."

I let myself relax into our bed, relishing in the slow, hot mouth that continued to lave every inch my skin. My lips quirked. He was right about one thing.

I was going to say yes.

Epilogue

Asher

It was all perfect.

The house, the candles, even the weather was cooperating and cast a warm, orange light over the brick exterior of our new home. My phone beeped, alerting me to the fact that my wife was almost here. There were perks to my job and being able to still keep track of her was my favorite.

Grinning, I hopped down the steps, closing the door behind me with a flourish and looked back on my handiwork.

I'd done a damn fine job, if I could say so myself. The front door had a massive white bow on the door. From every street facing window, soft candles glowed. The house looked warm, welcoming.

She was going to absolutely freak out.

I couldn't wait.

Wiping my sweating hands against my dress pants, I stood, eyes trained on the street. The SUV rounded the corner and pulled up in front of me. Anxiety pulled in my belly, but I shoved it down as I went to open the car door. Inside, as promised, was my angel.

"Hello, my love," I whisper against her hair, my hands guiding her out.

"If this is your version of a kidnapping, it is either going exceedingly well, or very poorly. I'm not sure." Lillian brushed a finger over the blindfold that I'd asked our driver to give her, the bright light from her wedding ring blinking back at me as she stepped to the sidewalk.

"I don't need to steal what's already mine?" I croon at her, slipping a hand around her waist, the other in her hand to guide her forward.

She takes about three steps before she slams on the breaks, halting us both. "Oh my god, Asher, if this is some kind of kink thing, I'm going to murder you for involving Timothy," even blindfolded my sweet Lillian glances back towards the driver.

I chuckle at her accusation, but don't go into detail about the strange situations that Timothy had picked us up in before. She didn't need to know those stories tonight.

Another time, perhaps.

"It's not a kink thing, unless you consider making my wife happy is a kink." I press her forward.

She moves along, letting me guide her up the five stairs until I hold her fast against me at the top.

My heart beats double time.

"Lillian, before I let you take this off, I have to tell you something." She turns towards me, her blind faith making my face ache as I smile.

"You are the most important thing in my world. I live to see you smile and crave you when you aren't near. I love you more than I thought I'd love anyone."

I pause, my throat suspiciously dry. I clear it once and her hand flutters up my chest to press into my face. "Asher…"

"No, no," I capture her hands and bring them to my mouth. "Let me get this out. Before I met you, I never thought I'd want this life. I never thought I'd want a home, a family, or even a wife. And now, I can't live without you. So please, start this next journey with me."

Lillian was completely still as my words settled over the pair of us. Slowly, carefully, I reach over and slip the blindfold down.

"Welcome home."

Lillian's eyes leave my face to glance over at the door to the side of us. "Asher. What? I thought that it was outbid."

I shrugged, her obvious joy making it nearly impossible to keep still. I wanted to show her everything. The master bedroom I would ravish her in. The bedrooms I wanted to fill with our babies. The kitchen we would pointlessly argue with.

"It was. I made it worth the next owner to step aside."

"I can't believe it," Lillian's fingers dropped to the door handle, and she froze looking back at me. "May I?"

"It's all yours."

Her smile lit me from the inside out. "Ours."

With a squeal, she pushed inwards and led the way back into this next chapter of our lives. After two laps through every room, I managed to slow her down, capturing her hand and pressing her back against the front door, letting the perfect weight of her body settle into my hands as I lifted her.

With a happy little moan, her hands found my shoulder and legs wrapped eagerly around my waist.

"You really love it?"

"I do," she purred, leaning in to press her lips against the side of my neck. Heat blooms there and my cock thickens immediately. My hunger for this sweet, dark creature was endless and now that I had her here in our new home, I couldn't stop myself from rocking against her body.

"You know, I thought that you were going to say something else," Lillian said, peppering more kisses up and down my jawline. I lean my head back to accommodate her actions. "With your speech and everything."

"My proclamation you mean?" I growl as her mouth gets a little more aggressive. "What do you think I could've been talking about?"

I can feel the little lift in her body as she takes a huge breath in. I pull back and let our eyes meet.

"Lillian?"

She shifts against me, her legs squeezing. "It's in my waistband." Her cheeks pinked a little. "I wasn't sure how I was going to…"

My fingers swept over the curve of her ass to where the waistband of her yoga pants and met warm, soft skin. Brows furrowed, I pulled back to tease her about sticking things down her pants, when I feel it.

Slender, only a few inches long, I maneuver the plastic out into the light of our new living room. Lilian was so slight I could really hold her with one arm, which was good, because suddenly I needed my other hand to bring the life-changing piece of medical equipment closer to my face.

I couldn't breathe, every cell in my body humming with overwhelming energy as I looked it over. Again, and again.

"I–," my voice broke. "Is this what I think it is?"

Lillian bit her lip, then nodded.

Elation blew through me like a firework and suddenly I couldn't get her close enough. "You're pregnant?"

She nodded, her face tucking into my neck again as I held her tight to my chest, unable to tear my eyes away from the test in my hand.

"How? When? Are you–," my words came in a rush, and I didn't care enough to repeat myself? She understood me, she always has.

Lillian gave a soft laugh, her breath warm on my skin. "The usual way. I just found out on Monday. And Asher–Asher I'm so happy. But I need to make sure you are too."

I dropped her legs from my waist, pushing back from my wife, my life as I fell to my knees. "Happy? Lillian, this is the greatest gift I've ever been given. I'm fucking elated."

Her laughter was music in my ears as I reached for her body. My fingers shook as I slowly pushed up her t-shirt and snagged the edge of her yoga pants to pull them low on her pelvis.

I stared.

Right there, right under my touch our baby was growing. The thought was enough to make foreign hot tears prick at the backs of my eyelids. I leaned in, pressing my lips there, feeling the firm, flat skin there.

You are so loved, I said with my kiss, projecting the thoughts as hard as I could at our future. "I can't wait to meet you."

Gentle hands caught in my curls and tugged my head back, so I was looking up into Lillian's tear-filled eyes. "We have a little time before that."

I rose slowly, my hands following the curves of her body. "A little time?"

She cocked her head playfully. "A little."

I reached down to cup her ass again, picking her up once again. "Whatever shall we do?"

Lillian's hands found my face and dragged it low. "I don't know, but I'm sure we'll think of something."

The End

NEXT IN THE SERIES
His to Keep
Emerson meets his match.

OTHER BOOKS BY GENNI BEE

Steamy Shorts (Trio #1)
His to Have
His to Hold
With His Ring

Steamy Shorts (Trio #2)
His to Love
His to Protect
His to Keep

Public Relations Series
The Playboy Project
The Unplanned Project
The Practice Project
The Protection Project (coming fall 2023)

Kismet Series
New Year's Kismet
Could Be Kismet (coming early 2023)

ACKNOWLEDGEMENTS

A huge thank you to all my readers and those who have enjoyed my stories.

KEEP IN TOUCH

Like her Facebook Page
Find her on TikTok
Follow her on Instagram
Follow her on Amazon
Follow her on Bookbub

ABOUT THE AUTHOR

Genni Bee lives in the Midwest with her spouse, two awesome kids, and a cat who thinks he's a dog. She loves swoon-worthy, dirty-talking heros and heroines who know what they want.

A note from the author:

Nothing would be possible without the immense help that I received from my friends, my family, my wonderful beta readers (especially W.C. who has been with me since book) and a team of very patient editors. Thank you all so very much.

Don't ever quit,
Genni Bee

Made in the USA
Coppell, TX
29 October 2023